THUNDER BRAKES

The February blizzard was raging around the little depot of Blue Buttes like a wild monster. 'Tex' Rankin, a tall, sinewy fellow and his cowboy partner, the earnest Dell Young, were awaiting the midnight train to whisk them down south. The snow was slapping against the waiting room and Tex just couldn't refrain from shivering. Then the blizzard blew in a slim young girl, June Hale, who wanted two men to help on her ranch, the Curly Q, while she went to attend to her injured father. Moved by her plight, Tex and Dell agreed, and watched her board the train going south—and then they heard that the Curly Q was about to go under!

THUNDER BRAKES

Cherry Wilson

First published 1929

This hardback edition 1997
by Chivers Press
by arrangement with
Golden West Literary Agency

ISBN 0 7451 4706 2

British Library Cataloguing in Publication Data available

Printed and bound in Great Britain by
Redwood Books, Trowbridge, Wiltshire

CONTENTS

CONTENTS

THUNDER BRAKES

CHAPTER I

"TILL KINGDOM COME!"

LIKE some wild, berserk monster the February blizzard was raging about the little depot of Blue Buttes—a flag stop in the far-flung Okanogan's Thunder River cattle range. Snow slapped against the heavily frosted panes of the waiting room. It whizzed through cracks below door and window ledge, where it piled up in little windrows of silver that jiggled and gleamed in the glow of the depot lamp. And all the air without was filled with the storm's wild shrieks; even the cheery *click, click, click,* of the telegraph key was howled down.

Within, two passengers awaited the midnight local that was to whisk them south. Cowboys they were, and partners. For their luggage—consisting of a suit case and saddle each—flaunted the Broken Bit brand.

One, "Tex" Rankin, was a tall, sinewy, keen-eyed fellow, with a lean, dark face. There was in it a brooding, haunting sadness, the light of some soul hunger, coupled with a restraint that made him a mysterious figure to stranger and to friend.

Even to his partner, Dell Young, Tex was a mystery. That there were secret places in Tex's heart locked to him, Dell instinctively knew. But he accepted his exclusion, only too proud and thankful to have the rest of Tex's heart. For Dell was the quiet, sincere sort that gives all and asks little—not, by any means, that it was little Dell got from Tex!

Straight and slim, of average height, Dell was a typical range rider. His face was open, boyish, bronzed. His eyes, blue-gray, earnest, were clear as mountain springs. One physical feature, and one only, he had in common with his partner—a slow, infrequent, but most engaging grin.

And he was grinning at Tex now, as he rose from the hard bench to stretch his legs and yawn, and so fight off the inclination for slumber brought on by the lateness of the hour, the tedium of the wait, and the monotonous moaning of the storm.

"We're sure gittin' a grand send-off, Tex!" he said, as the blizzard struck the depot a particularly vicious blast.

"If ever we git South," vowed Tex Rankin, in a slow, tooth-chattering, but unmistakably Texan drawl, "I know one hombre it won't git another whack at!"

Emptying the scuttle of coal in the stove, Tex poked up the drafts and humped himself over the roaring fire, his six-feet-two one long, recurrent shiver. "What if the train's snowed in somewhere?" he worried. "It's past due now. What if we're stalled here on this iceberg all night? Dell, I c-can't stand much more! Right now I'm froze that stiff you could drive me in the ground for a fence post!"

With this pitious declaration he shivered and shook in a way that would have presaged a mortal illness in another man, but which, in Tex, only made Dell's grin the broader.

For Tex had been shivering like that ever since the first cold snap last fall. He was a Texan, and this was his first real winter. The cold "got" him! He couldn't seem to put on clothes enough to keep warm. Couldn't get acclimated. The only times Dell had seen him halfway comfortable was when, over on the Broken Bit, he'd built up a fire that ran everybody else out of the bunk house—just as he had stoked this one, till the depot was like a baking oven—and stood over it, as he was standing now, his sheepskin coat and chaps smoking, and even his eyebrows singed.

"What's your religion, Tex?" one of the Broken Bit boys once asked him, when they were all expecting to see him go up in instantaneous combustion.

"Search me," Tex had drawled innocently. "Why?"

"Reckoned you was a fire worshiper!"

"Nope," put in another waddy when the laugh died down. "Tex is one of them vestal virgins what never lets the fire go out!"

The boys had joshed Tex a lot. But they'd been sorry for him, and sorry to see him go. Glad, too, for he was going home to Texas, "out of his misery," as he said. Dell, though, couldn't help feeling a little blue. He was going with Tex, because they were the kind of pals who couldn't part, but the Northwest was *his* home range, and——

The station agent, bringing in more fuel, looked dumfoundedly at the sizzling Texan, and inquired of Dell:

"What in Sam Hill is this pard of yours made of?"

Dell was used to the query and the awed look that accompanied it.

"Asbestos!" he grinned, dragging his saddle to the draftiest corner and straddling it there. "Heat don't penetrate Tex. Why, over on the Broken Bit we used to set him up behind the stove to keep the bunk-house wall from scorchin'! Yeah, he come in right handy, till we burned up the forest reserve. Then he seen his finish, an' beat it for the land of mesquite, scorpions, an' eternal heat!"

The agent cast a disapproving eye at Tex. "Don't like our climate, huh?"

Tex shuddered. "Yeah," he said with fine sarcasm, "it's a fine climate! Jist one thing I got agin' it—there's two or three months in the summer when the sleighin' gits thin! Say, how much longer we got to wait?"

"Not much," the agent assured him. "She's cleared Tyee." Then, being a loyal Okanoganer himself, and hating to see two such fine, upstanding young citizens leaving his section, he asked Dell:

"Why *you* leavin' God's country?"

"To save his life!" Dell nodded toward Tex. "He wouldn't go without me, an' I couldn't see him freeze. So where he goes, I go, an' his people shall be my people, for better or worse, till the sands of the desert grow cold!"

"Which I sure appreciate, Dell," Tex declared fervently, when the agent had been called back to the clicking key. "I'd 'a' froze like a man, before I'd ever have parted trails with you. But your goin' along makes everything jake. You won't be sorry, Dell. Not when you git down to Texas, where the sun don't lay down on the job half the year, an' a hombre's warm always an' natural—Lordy, I'll be bawlin' like a weanin' calf! Homesick, I reckon."

Rising, Dell went to the window, and scraping a little panel free from frost, gazed out at the night.

"Yeah," he said moodily; "reckon this time next year, I'll be homesick for snow."

"My gosh!" gasped Tex.

As if this supposition were quite the most singular thing in the world, he continued to stare at his partner in something between astonishment and horror, until Dell turned abruptly.

"Tex," asked the cowboy seriously, coming back to the fire, "how come you ever jarred loose from Texas in the first place? Was it jist foot itch brought you

North, or—— Don't tell me, Tex," he interrupted himself to protest, as swift-dawning pain shadowed the Texan's face. "Don't—if you'd rather not!"

For a long moment Tex Rankin was silent. He seemed far from Dell then, far even from the mournful wailing of the storm.

"It ain't no secret," he said at last, the light of some hungry longing looking out of his eyes at Dell, "leastwise, it's nothing I can't tell free—tell *you.* But it's a family matter, an' it hurts—heaps. Some day, Dell, I want you to know. But now—when I'm leavin'—I'd rather jist forget it, if it's all the same."

Dell's hand went to Tex's shoulder in a gesture of rare affection. "Sure," he said quietly, "we'll forget it. But if ever I can help, Tex—well, you know you can count on me."

The Texan's lithe, brown fingers closed on Dell's hand in a grip of iron, and heart-deep was his answer, "I sure do!"

For these two were partners in no ordinary sense of the word. No mutual need or convenience had brought them together, and held them there. Nor had they merely become a habit with each other through a long, close intimacy of years. Theirs was simply the love of man for man—a relationship as old as man, and perhaps man's noblest. Not that they ever moralized about it.

They had met, under dramatic circumstances, down in the Yakima country the spring before. And on the instant of their meeting, something had sprung up between them that it would be hard for man to break. Man! Could woman break it? Should they have the misfortune to love the same woman, would that part them? Would such a friendship be put to that test of tests? It would! For——

Straight through the storm, forcing her horse through the drifts at a perilous pace, in a desperate effort to beat the midnight local in, she was coming!

All unaware of her very existence, they got their luggage in a convenient heap by the door. Trains stopped with scant formality at Blue Buttes, as if they disdained to stop at the little cow town at all, but paused in passing, as poises a bird on the wing.

The blizzard shook the depot with a fury that made the very clapboards ring.

"Great post holes!" cussed the Texan, ignoring the fact that man proposes, but God disposes. "I wouldn't stay in this forsaken, froze-up country, if you give it to me! I'd rather be in Hades! Sam Houston, I'll say I would! For then I'd stand a tolerable show of gittin' war——"

The depot door burst open, and the blizzard blew her in!

A slim little thing, she was, and might have been fashioned from the very winter Tex condemned. Her short, dark cloak was a gleaming sheet of snow. Her tight, little hat, a cap of glittering crystals, from under which snow-powdered curls escaped. And her face, seen in a fleeting glimpse as she rushed to the ticket window, was white as any new-blown drift.

"Good heavens!" they heard the agent cry out as he saw her. "How did you make it? I never dreamed you'd come through that!"

"Then I'm in time?" and the cowboys knew she had not left the storm outside.

"In the very nick of it! The train's late."

Either from relief or weariness, she swayed. "Thank goodness!" and her voice was fiercely glad. "Any message come since, Lem?"

"Not any," denied the agent, as though glad of it. "Lucky I caught a ranger ridin' your way, or no tellin' when you'd have got that one. Now, don't you worry," he said kindly, punching a ticket to a destination which, certainly, she had not named. "The wire said 'injured.' It didn't say 'seriously.' An' if your dad had been hurt bad, they'd have worded it that a way—they always do. Jeff Hale——"

Tex Rankin started; then froze in his tracks—and not from cold!

"Jeff ain't the kind that kills easy," solaced the agent. "How's things at the Curly Q?"

"They couldn't be worse," the girl said wearily. Then, switching the theme with an abruptness that took their breath, "Lem, what's your idea of hell?"

"Fire an' brimstone," he readily defined for all his wonder, "with a lot of long-tailed imps herdin' the wicked with two-tined forks."

"You're wrong," she said bitterly. "It's winter on a cattle ranch, with no feed!"

"Sho!" The agent looked grave. "It can't be that bad!"

"Just about! We've got hay for a week, by stretching it out. But I almost wish we hadn't—for it's slow torture. We've starved them through, praying for an early Chinook, and now this storm——" Her voice faltered and broke. "Even if we had feed, Lem, we'll have no one to give it out soon! Calliope and Dutch are dead on their feet. Why, Hector's the best man of the three! I counted fifteen cows down this morning——"

"Where's Bannock?"

"Gone over to the enemy."

"The infernal ol' traitor!" exclaimed the agent with heat.

The girl shrugged listlessly. "Oh, you can't blame him, Lem. You can't expect a cowhand to work like a dog for thirty dollars a month, when he can get sixty just to fool around the Box Bar—not when he's old. Rush Kinney knows—and, God forgive him, none knows better—the fix we're in. If we can't pull the herd on Thunder Brakes we're lost. And we can't without men. Now, with dad hurt——"

"Get men," struck in the agent, moved by a strong desire to help.

"Where?" she challenged, with a despairing little gesture.

By merest chance his gaze fell on the two punchers listening shamelessly.

"Right behind you," he said hurriedly, "there's two waddies waitin' to take the train out. They're billed through to Texas. But I'd size them up as hombres what would discommode themselves to help a lady—sayin' you can thaw the big one out! But they ain't the kind your dad hires an'——"

Whatever he meant by that, Dell and Tex were left to wonder, for the girl had whirled on them. And the sun of the lamp, shining on the rain of melted snow that gemmed her garments, made a hundred little rainbows, through which she moved toward them. The sun of hope in her blue eyes, starred with tears—or melted flakes that lingered on her lashes, still—gave them the glorious brilliance of the rainbow, through which her stark appeal shone out.

Their eyes returned her gaze as tensely—Dell's, warm, gray, friendly; Tex Rankin's, blazing with a nameless fire that burned her through and through. And, though it was at Dell that women were wont to look first and longest, it was on Tex that the gaze of this girl fixed in desperate appeal.

"Boys——".

Faint, but clarion clear to nerves long strained for it, the shriek of the midnight local was borne down the gale!

"Boys"—in very desperation now—"do you want a job?"

Beauty in distress—and, despite the ravages of grief and care and toil, she was more than beautiful—appeals to any cowboy. But no woman had ever made, *could* make, that same appeal to Dell. Somehow, he realized it then. He wanted to offer himself, started to, but in the act remembered Tex. Tex wouldn't stay here, if you gave him the State! Tex was going South, and he'd promised——

"No, don't answer yet!" She must be honest, even in the press of time and need. "Do you want a job where you'll have to do three men's work? Work day and night, with no hope of relief? Take chances on your wages and chances of another kind that I cannot name! And, if you do—can I trust you? Will you stick?"

Astoundingly, with a hoarse violence no less startling, "Till kingdom come!" cried Tex.

Jerked out of the daze into which that threw him, by the sharp urgence of a second whistle, more loud and shrill, Dell reminded his partner: "But you're goin'——"

"Not for a minute!" Tex nudged him meaningly, as all three moved toward the door. "My folks was Eskimos, I was born in an igloo, an' raised on icicles, so I'm right at home here!"

Then they were on the platform, being mercilessly buffeted by the storm. And the girl had clasped an arm of each, and was raising herself on tiptoe, that she might be heard above the roar of the gale and the rumble of the oncoming train.

"I'm June——"

"Girl, I knew it!" Tex broke in huskily.

"You knew it?" She expressed the wonder Dell could only look.

"I—I knew June had come!" Tex stammered clumsily in cowboy gallantry. "Here I been laborin' under the delusion it was February, till you——"

"I'm June Hale, of the Curly Q, twelve miles south of Blue Buttes." Swift, clipped, her speech must be, for the local was grinding alongside. "My father went to Spokane last week on business. I've just got word he's been hurt. I don't know how, or how bad, but I'm going to him. I'll be back as soon as ever I can. Go right out to the ranch. You'll find things in a mess there. But if you're the kind of men I take you for, you'll know what to do. I don't ask the impossible of you, but—— Oh, keep things together somehow, till I come!"

The stool was down, and her little riding boot was on it.

"Please take my horse out." She waved toward the little pony, waiting dispiritedly in the snow and dark.

From the vestibule she leaned down with a last entreaty: "Be patient with Hector, boys. He's a trial sometimes, but he's a dear!"

Then, as the train gave a mighty lurch: "God bless you both!"

She was gone. She might never have been. They might have dreamed her, but for the fact that they were here, left high and dry, figuratively speaking, by this swift reversal of their plans. They stood there on the depot platform, staring with snow-stung eyes at the disappearing train—the whole tenor of their lives changed, sentenced by their own consent to hard labor, instead of being on the train, luxuriously speeding south.

Dell's mind was a fog of bewilderment, through which two inextinguishable queries pierced. Why weren't they the kind her father hired? And—who was Hector? The best man on the ranch! The last man in her thoughts!

"Pard"—at that plaintive drawl Dell became acutely conscious of Tex—"she's struck me all of a heap. I don't know which way from me is, if any! I—I'm all a-tremble, Dell!"

"You're cold," Dell said mechanically.

Fiercely Tex denied it. "I'm hot!" he cried tensely. "Hot all over!"

And Dell remembered, with no element of humor in the memory, that from the instant Tex had seen June Hale, he hadn't shivered once!

CHAPTER II

"BAT" ROUGE

THAT his partner's warmth was merely a state of mind, Dell soon knew, for almost in the same breath Tex was cussing the cold, snow, country, and all pertaining thereto. And, judging by his own emotions, Dell thought his change had been kindled solely by sympathy for the girl they were pledged to help. Yet so radical was the change in Tex, that Dell was suddenly in awe of him, as of a stranger.

"Now what?" he asked, and ever after it struck him queer how instinctively he reversed all precedence of their partnership by turning to Tex for guidance.

"Obey orders," Tex said tersely. "Take June's pony home. We'll stop in Blue Buttes jist long enough to rent another."

Returning to the depot to get their luggage and cash in on their tickets, the agent gave them a better idea of what they were up against.

"I'm afraid you boys won't thank me none for the job," he admitted frankly; "for the Curly Q's about to go under. You heard what June said—no feed, no men. I heard Hale took the last cent he could scrape up down to Spokane in the hope of buyin' hay there. But it's a lost bet, for there's no hay to be bought in the Northwest this year.

"An', as if this ain't trouble enough, there's a feud of a year's standing between the Curly Q an' Box Bar. Can't say what started it—some ol' grudge between Rush Kinney an' Jeff Hale—but you'll be in on the finish. For the Curly Q's got to put its herd on Thunder Brakes or lose it, an' the Box Bar will fight that tooth an' nail!"

"What's Thunder Brakes?" Tex had listened with strange intensity.

Nonplused, the agent rumpled his hair. "Blessed if I know!" he confessed. "Funny how much a hombre thinks he knows till he comes to tell it! But it's a kind of no-man's-land between the two ranches. Both claim it. The Box Bar does so, because Kinney's homesteaded it; an' the Curly Q, because Hale's got it leased. Though how to reconcile them facts, is too much for a Jim Hill man.

"Anyhow, there's a grand battle comin' off when the Curly Q herd goes on. Hale will put it on, or die tryin', for his back's to the wall—— Wrong again! Hale's flat on his back down in Spokane, an' it's your fight!"

To Dell, there seemed more than the loyalty of the cowboy, who, having sworn allegiance to one brand, matter of factly takes its quarrels upon himself, in Tex's answer:

"I'm spoilin' for a fight!"

"Then here's a tip." Confidentially, the agent leaned nearer. "Keep your eye on Bat Rouge. He's the Box Bar foreman, an' Rush Kinney's Man Friday! He prides himself on bein' the best scrapper on this range, an' he's crooked as a dog's hind leg. Not everybody knows it, but Bat's bad medicine!"

Dell was mulling this over as, leading the Curly Q horse, they battle the five long blocks uptown.

"A winter job on a cattle ranch, shy on men an' feed," he mused aloud, "is no cinch at best. But with prospects of a range fight——"

"It's a hot job, anyhow!" finished Tex, with a satisfaction that completely silenced Dell.

What had come over Tex, he wondered, that he could forget how cold he had been, could volunteer for a hard job like that? Of course, he had, too—but that was different. He didn't mind winter. He'd just been going, to be with Tex. But Tex—— It couldn't be *all* sympathy for June. What was it? Had Tex fallen in love with June?

He had his partner's own word for it that she had struck him "all in a heap." And he recalled now, with some feeling sharp as pain, that she had been no less impressed by Tex. But could love do that—spring up all in flower at just one glance, one word? And suddenly Dell knew it could! Knew forcibly that *he* loved her!

"She's mighty sweet!" Tex said patly out of the gloom.

"She sure is, Tex."

Even as Dell agreed, a blinding flash played on his mind, in which he seemed to glimpse all the black misery to come. And in the light of that revelation, in his great affection for Tex, he almost wished he had never seen June Hale!

"Tex," pain and fear wrung from him, "this ain't the rock on which we're goin' to split?"

Startled, Tex asked: "Which?"

"Us both thinkin' June Hale's sweet!"

Oh, sweet to Dell was Tex's low laugh, then! "Not a chance!"

But still Dell wasn't content. "Sure, pard?"

Touched by the boy's appeal, Tex stepped closer. Words were trembling on his lips—words that would have spared them all—but the old habit of silence ruled.

"Dell," he said, with a solemnity that made the words a mockery in days to come, "there ain't many things in this world that's sure—but you can be *dead* sure of that!"

Truer than truth to Dell was Tex's word, and his heart was light, and his feet felt not the weight of snow.

"Besides," Tex added queerly, "there's Hector. He's a trial sometimes, but he's a dear!"

Dell swore with a savage force that must have been a revelation itself to Tex, "*Dang* Hector!"

It was well after one in the morning, and Blue

Buttes was long asleep. But enough light penetrated the dingy window of the livery barn to show that some one was on duty there, and eventually their vigorous pounding brought him to the door. He was a goggle-eyed splinter of a man, whose nood nature had not been disturbed by this late call, though it was plain his slumber had.

"Hosses? Sure, Mike!" he yawned. "I'll saddle 'em up, an' trot 'em out. But, good grief"—suddenly jerking wide awake—"you don't aim to travel in this storm!"

With some impatience, Tex admitted that they did.

"In a rush, huh?" Curiosity was the stableman's besetting sin, and "Curious," his range name.

"Kind of."

"To git somewheres?"

"Yeah." Tex admitted that, too, grinning in spite of himself. "If it'll help any to git us started, I don't mind tellin' you. We're goin' to the Curly Q. Hired out there."

"Curly Q!" gasped the stableman, goggle-eyed in all truth. "You've been hired—to—work—for—the —Curly Q?"

"What's so queer about that?" demanded Tex; but he got no reply.

Speechlessly, the man held up his lantern and studied their faces, at the same time revealing to them the downright disbelief on his own. Then, shaking his head and mumbling to himself, as if the circumstance of their being employed by the Curly Q was too much to contemplate if sanity was to be preserved, he led the way to a near-by stall.

Here, speechless still, he hung the lantern on a peg, slipped in beside a feeding pinto, and was backing him out, when a man rode into the barn—a big, dark-faced, bold-eyed puncher on a high-spirited black. He came in like he owned the earth, thought Dell. And he'd come far, for snow clung in balls to the long wool of his flashy, red chaps. Knew the stableman, too, for he familiarly greeted him:

" 'Lo, Curious!"

And, as if he must share the burden or burst, Curious pointed to them and gasped: "They're—goin'—to —work—for—the Curly Q!"

Like forked lightning, the newcomer's eyes darted their way. Suddenly, Dell was aware of a strange tension in the air. He felt it increase, as the man dismounted and swaggered up, slapping his snowy sombrero against his chaps. Now, as he stepped under the lantern, Dell saw the man's face more distinctly, and liked it less, though it was plain he was pleased with it himself. For there was amazing self-assurance in the way his bold eyes swept Dell and Tex from head to foot, missing nothing in that one glance.

"Curly Q, huh?" His tone was neutral at least. "Boys, you're makin' a bad bet. That outfit's on its last legs. If you're lookin' for work, you'd better hook up with the Box Bar. We can always use good men, an' I'll guarantee top wages, good chuck——"

"Work there yourself, mebbe?" softly insinuated Tex, who had been doing some surveying himself.

"Foreman there," chestily owned the puncher.

They knew then that this was Bat Rouge, their inherited enemy—"bad medicine," the agent had warned them! Looking quickly at Tex, Dell saw that little throat muscle dance, an infallible sign of rising excitement.

"Yeah, you'd better tie up with us," advised the foreman, more sure of his ground. "Jeff Hale's on the rocks. You'd be out of a job in two weeks' time."

"How come?" drawled Tex, yet more softly. "I understand Hale's herd can be saved, if it's put on Thunder Brakes."

Bat Rouge started. *"If!"* he jeered, his face working with some nameless emotion. "That's a mighty big little word! Who's goin' to put it on—with me an' my men ridin' fence to see they don't?"

"We'll put it on," Tex enlightened him quietly, "if Hale wants it there! You tell Rush Kinney that the Curly Q's took a new lease on life. An' while it may be short-handed now, it'll have a full house when we git there! Tell him that, Bat!"

Too choked by fury to adequately express himself, Bat grated: "It won't be worth while!"

"I'll try to make it worth your while!"

Even Dell, who knew how indescribably reckless Tex could be, was startled by that soft promise.

Again Bat sized him up from head to heel, and, with some dire premonition, so terribly prophetic, Dell's eye took the measure of both men. They were big, powerful, quick-moving men. And while Tex had a little the better of it in height, Bat's was the more rugged and muscular build.

"You might at that," Bat grudgingly admitted, "an' I hope it comes to that! But you didn't git me. I meant it wouldn't be worth while to relay your message. For June Hale must have hired you, an' while"—some passion darkened his face, envenomed his tone, and just to hear her name on his lips made Dell see red—"while you may be *her* idea of a cow-hand——"

"Easy, Bat!" drawled Tex, in a tone that made Dell's blood tingle, though he had heard it a time or two before.

It had the same effect on Bat, for he finished civilly enough:

"It's dollars to doughnuts you won't be there long, after Jeff Hale gits back! You ain't the kind *he* hires!"

What the deuce did he mean by that? The agent had said the same thing. What kind did Jeff Hale hire?

"What kind are *we?*" Dell asked Tex, when, riding June's pony beside Tex's rented pinto, they passed through the sleeping town. "I'd say we was up to the average, an' over. What's wrong with us?"

"Too deep for me," Tex said tersely. "But we'll stay!"

He spoke with so much conviction that Dell glanced at him sharply.

Tex was bent over his horse's neck, intently scanning some small object in his hand, by the light of the last street lamp.

"What you got there, Tex?"

"Train check," said the laconic puncher, holding it out to Dell. "Our friend Bat knocked it out of his hat when he was dustin' the snow off. Reckon he didn't come by hoss—all the way!"

Dell glanced casually at the little green strip of pasteboard. It was the regulation check, marked and punched, that conductors exchange for tickets, for their own identification of passengers. Dell was surprised at how carefully Tex returned it to his pocket, and straightway lapsed into a silence unbroken for miles.

Moving beside Tex, head bowed to the snow-freighted wind, Dell's thoughts flashed like summer lightning through his mind. Why did Bat Rouge hate June? No feud could account for the hatred he had shown! Where had Bat been? How had Jeff Hale been hurt? Why were folks so sure he wouldn't have hired them? Why was Tex so sure they'd stay?

He had the bewildering feeling that much that was dark to him was clear as day to Tex, but he rejected the thought. For Tex had never been within a hundred miles of Blue Buttes, until to-day, when they'd come in on the stage to take the train.

Out on the open highway, where the wind got a full swing at them, and the snow was piled at times in breast-high drifts, rode Dell Young and Tex Rankin, for weary mile on mile. Dell marveled that June had come through that heavy snow, even when using whip and spur; while Tex, through drawn lips and pounding teeth, cussed every inch of it. It comforted Dell to hear Tex cuss snow. For it sounded like Tex, and was about his only utterance that did.

Now the hills closed in, black with fir and pine, as down the somber gorge they rode, into the heart of Thunder River Range. Often a coyote's howl rang down the hills, quavering, and sweetly shrill—a sound Dell had always loved, as symbolic of the wild land he loved. When its voice was heard no longer in the land, the land would be no longer wild. But, strangely now, it sent a chill creeping through his veins, as if, in that wild and haunting cry had materialized and spoken all the hunger, cold, and anguish of the frozen range!

CHAPTER III

HECTOR

DAY was breaking, cold and gray, when they rode over a high rise and looked down upon a ranch in a sheltered valley, which, from the agent's description, they knew must be the Curly Q. The low, rambling, log ranch house, barns, and corrals, were grouped on a high crown of land, from which the valley dipped away to the broken, timbered hills.

Seen in summer, the beauty of its setting would have thrilled them—with Thunder River flashing, singing; and all the countless little leaves in the fringing willows, atwinkle and ashine; and the fragrant flowers of thickets and meadowland.

But now the willows lifted wintry boughs and made melancholy moaning. The thickets were naked. Frozen the stream, and hushed. All was cold and dead, as though the girl—whose eyes, Dell thought, must have taken their blue from the columbine that summered here—had lost her fight, and the snow, thick strewn on all, was the white ashes of her every hope.

Riding under the high-arched gate, they pulled up before the house, eagerly anticipating fire and food after their night ride through the storm. But no one came in answer to their knocking, which echoed eerily through the deserted rooms. Nor was there any sign of life about the corrals. Nor even at the barn, where they turned the horses in. Coming out, standing there uncertain, a deep depression settled over Dell.

"It—it gives me the creeps," he said shakily. "It's so spooky and still. A ghost ranch sure!"

Tex said strangely: "It's sure a cold reception, Dell!"

Exploring farther, they heard a dismal lowing. And, following the sound to the brow of a wind-protected vale behind the barn, they stopped, rooted in the snow, stunned by the seriousness of the job they had so impulsively undertaken. For now, face to face with it, they saw the hopelessness of the situation they had come to save.

Spread out below them were the feed yards, covering several acres—a crisscross of fences, constructed of huge logs. Long, low, brush-thatched sheds of poles had been built for shelter. And long feeding racks sprawled over the yards. Over the whole, filling their stricken eyes to the exclusion of all else, was the Curly Q herd.

That herd! No words could depict it—the sorriest herd upon which Dell or Tex had ever looked. Some five hundred cows in every degree of starvation. Starved through! They showed it! In rough, gaunt flanks, that even the snow, caked thickly in their long hair, could not fill.

In protruding ribs, and weaving limbs, they showed it. In the way they staggered and stopped, milling without aim or purpose, seeking something that was not there. Searching for it with dead, dull eyes in drooping heads. Those that had stood it best, crowded about the racks, sniffing with frosted nostrils for a stray spear of hay. Calves bawled piteously. All lowed monotonously.

Yet not all! For some had not the life to mill or bawl, but lay like dead upon the trampled snow, waiting stolidly for death. Of these, June had counted fifteen the morning before. Dell counted twenty now. And he, with the experience of many severe winters on which to base his judgment, wondered if Tex could possibly appreciate what the Curly Q was up against. For Tex's experience with winter was limited to this one on the Broken Bit, where every cow could founder herself daily, and make no great inroad on the store of hay.

Looking about for the Curly Q hay, he saw the pitiful remnant of a stack, stoutly fenced from the hungry herd. Short of feed, indeed, if this were all! "I almost wish it was"—Dell remembered June Hale's cry—"for it's slow torture!"

Glancing now at Tex, he saw the big fellow's dark gaze go to the hay, come back to the miserable herd, and swing to the "down" cows. More now than on the day before, and, if help were not forthcoming, there would be more to-morrow, and the next day, and the next——

"Hell ain't in it!" muttered Tex.

Horror held them, heedless of chilled bodies, screened by a bare thicket from the view of two men working with the down cows below—the most arduous, exasperating work on a cattle ranch. For, once a cow has given up, she will make no move to help herself, but must be lifted bodily—often stubbornly insists upon being lifted, even after she has been fed back to strength.

Dell studied the men with interest. "If they're the kind Jeff Hale hires," he told Tex, "then we—ain't!"

These were old men—too old for such strenuous work—for their faces were gray and haggard, their bowed old legs unsteady. Yet in spirit and loyalty, how strong! For here they were "dead on their feet," doing the work of three men, taking chances on their wages——

"I hope we're half as good!" Tex said warmly.

And Dell, appreciatively watching their expert handling of a down cow, said no less warmly:

"They sure know their business, Tex!"

Grasping the horns of a prostrate cow, one old puncher hauled her around in a half upright position, and held her there while his companion worked the long pole he carried beneath her breast. Then, one at either end of the pole, their free hand steadying her, they lifted with all their strength, raising her front quarters high enough to enable them to place her forelegs under her.

Now, holding her in that position, each grasped a flank with his free hand and heaved with might and main, until the spirit moved the discouraged beast to hold up her own hind quarters with her own hind legs. Another heave at the pole, and she was on all four feet, swinging tremblingly, braced on both sides by the men.

Waiting a few moments, they forced her to take a few steps, until the blood was circulating and the worst numbness gone, when, of her own volition, she moved weakly toward the racks. And taking heart from the fact that she was up and doing, she turned on her benefactors, with the ungrateful display of temper characteristic of a range cow, and made a feeble, but spirited attempt to fight. Knowing it was safe to leave her now, the old fellows took up their pole and went on to the next.

This cow appeared totally lifeless to Dell and Tex. But some vital spark must have lingered, for one of the old-timers complained in tired and querulous tone:

"She ain't dead yet!"

"She's too danged ornery to die!" peevishly cussed the other. "I've h'isted her up an' down, day in an' day out, till I'm 'most on the lift myself!"

They studied her a moment in silence, then silently studied each other.

"They say," ruminated the first old puncher, "if you turn a down cow over, she'll die sure. Ever hear that, Dutch?"

"I've heered it," Dutch speculatively nodded. "Wonder if it works?"

Then, in complete, unspoken understanding, they stooped, and were in the very act of turning her over, when a small tornado swooped down out of nowhere, in the form of a white-faced, blazing-eyed boy of eleven or so.

"I heard you!" he shrilled at the conscience-stricken pair. "You—you double-crossin', back-bitin' sons of a mangy coyote!" His voice was hampered by tears and fury, but possessed of a surprising brilliance and fluency, nevertheless. "How can I watch the hay like I promised June, an' watch you, too! I can't be *everywheres!* An' the minit I turn my back, you start killin' my cows. Go on over to the Box Bar where you belong! I don't want a man on the place I can't trust. I—I'd a danged sight ruther go it alone!"

"It—it didn't work, son!" Dutch said sheepishly. "Thar, thar! Don't cry!"

"Who's cryin'?" demanded the youngster fiercely. "Can't you tell when a hombre's cryin', an' when he's mad! Of all the mean, sneakin' Bat Rouge tricks——"

His nerves, overstrung by a sense of responsibility too heavy for his years, caught the muffled footfalls of Dell and Tex advancing, and he whirled like a top. Seeing two strange men on the premises, he snatched up the pitchfork that lay at his feet, and presented it, business end first.

"Git back!" he shrilled, and if there were tears in his eyes, there was desperation, also, and a curious whiteness about mouth and nostrils that reminded Dell vividly of Tex in a dangerous mood.

"Stay back—or I'll punch the daylights outta you! Snoopin' around for Bat Rouge, are you? Tryin' to sneak up an' burn the rest of our hay! You know my dad's hurt, an' you think there ain't a man on the ranch!"

"We know there is, Bud," Tex said gently, coming steadily on. "Put it down."

But the boy's fingers tensed on the fork, with even more resolution, and his eyes fairly snapped. The hysteria with which he cried, as Tex came on in even strides: "I'll jab you! Honest to gosh, I will! I'm *warnin'* you!" gave Dell a more graphic idea of the cruel strain the Curly Q was under, than June's distress, Bat Rouge's vindictiveness, or anything that had gone before.

Dell wondered if the boy's spirit—of which it was plain the two old fellows stood in awe—was a true reflection of Jeff Hale's.

"Better put it down, Bud," Tex said softly. "You don't want to mutilate your new hands."

Surprise lowered the fork a trifle, but suspicion jerked it back.

"Tell another!" jeered the boy. "You're the kind of hombres *other* men hire—but not my dad!"

"We're hired, Bud."

"Since when?" derisively.

"Since midnight. Your sister hired us."

At that blessed news, one old puncher started a whoop he couldn't finish and collapsed in the snow. And the other, keening his old nose to the desolate sky, chanted, in inharmonious but prayerful thanksgiving:

"Praise God, from whom all blessin's flow,
Praise him, ye sinners here below——"

"Shut off the steam, 'Calliope'!" shrieked the other, scrambling stiffly to his feet. "An' shake hands with the reënforcements!"

"My name's Young," grinned Dell, wringing Dutch's horny old hand, "an' my pard, here——"

But Tex was kneeling in the snow, his long arms about the boy, who was now weeping frankly, soothing him with a gentleness of which no one but Dell would have believed him capable.

"You ain't a thing to worry about, now," he told the boy, with something in his tone that made Dell's eyes smart. "That's our job. The crew does the work, an' worryin', but a good boss looks after his men. Now, I'm froze that brittle, I'd break if you bent me, an' I'm plumb hollow clear to my toes. Reckon you could rustle us some coffee, Bud?"

The boy dashed his sleeve across his eyes, and lifted his eyes to Tex. Already the light of hero-worship was there—a light that never went out.

"Coffee!" he cried joyously. "Sure thing—in three shakes of a lamb's tail! Oh, gee, everything's hunky-dory—now I got *regular* men!"

He turned away, ran back, and caught Tex by the arm.

"Say," he confided then—and, oh, how *dear* Dell thought him—"I ain't Bud—I'm *Hector!*"

CHAPTER IV

FOREMAN, PRO TEM

"Oh, I come to a river, an' I couldn't git across,
Sing Polly Wolly Doodle all the day——"

OLD Calliope sang off key as usual, but with true grace notes of joy, as he poured a little water out of the teakettle over the old coffee grounds, and gave the pot a "swizzle" in the hope of extracting another cup.

"I jumped on a nigger, an' I thought he was a
hoss,
Sing——"

"Holy cow, don't!! Dutch pleaded. "Personally, I'm so happy right now I could endure anything, but the boys want to know what the situation is."

Instantly Calliope sobered. "They seen it," he said truly. "But I can sum it up for 'em in jist three words—starvation, demoralization, an' damnation!"

Dell and Tex, hearing this indorsement of their first impressions, were grave.

They had breakfasted well on Hector's coffee and

Calliope's flapjacks and bacon. And now, in the pleasant glow that comes of physical comfort and a heart-stirring welcome, sat before the big range in the Curly Q kitchen, ready—as Dell had told Dutch—to get down to brass tacks.

"Is that all the hay you got—what's left in that stack?" Tex, humped over the stove with his feet in the oven, straightened to ask.

"Except for a leetle hoss feed in the barn," said Calliope stonily, "it's all. An' all we'll git till more sprouts in due course of nature! Jeff's failin' to rustle any down in Spokane cooked the Curly Q's goose. For this here blizzard——"

"How come you to be in this shape?" Dell put in practically. "Didn't you put up hay to see you through?"

The effect of that was electrical. Both old punchers leaned tautly across the table. The boy, sticking like a bur to his hero, turned as tensely on Dell.

"Didn't we?" Calliope echoed, tremblingly raising a clenched old fist. "Didn't we have five big stacks an' a barnful?"

Naturally Dell asked, "Where did it go?"

That brought Cal's fist down with a bang, "Up in smoke!"

As startling to Dell, was the way Tex's feet came out of the oven, as he hitched around in his chair to watch Cal.

"One night last fall," quavered the old man in

holy wrath, "we'd jist got to bed, when some one yells, 'Fire!' An' we wake up to see a hellish red shine on the winder pane. By the time we got down there, the four meadow stacks was all in a blaze. An' there wasn't a gosh a'mighty thing we could do, but watch 'em burn, an' curse the black-hearted devil that done it!"

Tex's eyes were like flint. "Then you know who?" he asked.

Cal's tired old face was grim as he ominously responded: "We do! His hoss left tracks, an' I follered 'em straight to the Box Bar! When he got off his hoss there—which he took pains not to do *here*—I found the print of a No. 10 boot. There ain't but one man in this country got a understandin' that big—an' Bat Rouge is the man!"

Tex got up at that, and Dell, riled, too, by this outrage, watched him pace. At last, he turned tensely on Cal: "What did Hale do?" he asked.

"What *could* he do?" countered Calliope wearily. "Nobody *seen* him throw the match! We know he did it, but we can't prove it. No more'n we can prove any of the crooked deals they pulled off in this fuss, that led up from a chewin' match to the row over Thunder Brakes!"

"Jist what is Thunder Brakes?" Dell wanted to get at the heart of this plight.

"A fenced-in section between here an' the Box Bar." All the fire burned out of him, Calliope sank heavily back in his chair. "It ain't been ranged since Heck, here"—he waved toward the boy—"was a pup. Bunch grass is thick, an' there's patches of rye grass, acre wide an' man high. The wind blows a hurricane there, an' keeps it snow-free. An' our herd could live fat there till spring."

"Then why in the world," Tex demanded, recalling the state of the herd, ain't you put it on there?"

"Because Hale's lease don't go in effect till the first day of March," was the calm response.

While Tex darkly brooded on it, Dell put the question that the agent had found too much for a "Jim Hill man." "Whose land is it? How can the Curly Q lease it, an' the Box Bar homstead it, too?"

Together, one helping the other out, the old fellows told him.

Long ago, in the good old days, when both ranches had ranged their herds together, and there was never a fence between, nothing but neighborliness and good will, a nester, named McQuire, had squatted on Thunder Brakes. He built a cabin and fenced the land. But when surveyed, it was found to be in section 36, and so was school land—for every sixth and thirty-sixth section went to the State for that use.

The State contested McQuire's right to the land as a matter of form. But McQuire could have made his claim stick, on the grounds that he'd squatted on and improved the land before he knew it was State land, and the government would have given the State other land in lieu of it.

However, about that time Rush Kinney and Jeff Hale sprang their feud. What started it? Well, what starts any fuss? Human nature, Calliope reckoned, and human sin. Anyhow, it was a difference of opinion on what constituted that last, which started this one. Then Hale fenced in Cayuse Springs, barring Kinney from the best part of the range. And "some of that devil's tribe," meaning the Kinneys, bought McQuire's improvements and filed a homestead on Thunder Brakes, to acquire more range. But the Kinney filing was protested on grounds that the original settler's relinquishment made it State land again. Just the same, Kinney was hanging on up there, till his claim was thrashed out by law.

"When they burned our hay," Calliope concluded, "Jeff saw he had to range Thunder Brakes, or go smash. So he leased it from the State. Kinney goes hog wild when he hears it, an' swears he'll massacre the first Curly Q waddy to trespass up there! The sheriff refused to interfere none—it's outta the province of his office, he says, to decide which claim is right.

"Reckon, now, nobody'll ever be called on to decide it, for we won't have any herd left to put up there on March first! Jeff wires he can't scare up any hay in Spokane. Plop on that, comes a wire he's hurt——"

Tex swung again, in his restless pacing. "Reckon the Box Bar had a hand in that?"

"Waal"—it was hard for Cal to be dishonest—"an outfit what would burn another man's hay, would do anything! But Jeff was hurt in Spokane, an' the Box Bar's on Thunder River range."

The Texan smiled grimly. "Bat," he said, and his voice was grim, "has strayed off his range!" And he showed them the little green train check he'd retrieved from the stable floor after Bat had knocked it out of his hat.

The old fellows all but looked the spots off of it.

"Reckon we could find out from the agent, what them marks mean—where Bat's been," Cal conjectured, handing it over at last. "But, so far, we don't know how Jeff was hurt. Likely he tangled with one of them street cars—they're plumb ruinous to a range man. If he was hurt by a human, he'll know it, an' tell us when he gits back. I'd hang onto that check, Tex. But the question before the house now, is what to do with the herd!"

All this while, the boy had been shaking all over, couldn't keep still. And now he caught Tex by both hands, and frantically tugged them.

"Tex," he pleaded, his black eyes burning his white face up, "you'll put it on? You'll put our herd on Thunder Brakes, Tex?"

They saw the big Texan stiffen. Only Dell noticed that throat muscle dance. Only Tex, himself, knew how deep Hector's plea sank! But they all heard him recklessly vowing:

"I'll put it on!"

Fear, that was surely prescient, seized hard on Dell. They had no right, he cried earnestly, to plunge the Curly Q in a fight that must end in bloodshed without authority from Hale.

"If Hale comes home," he reasoned, blind to the boy's flashing scorn, "an' wants it on—all right! But not till then." And fear took a new grip, as he saw that Tex wasn't even listening to him.

Despairing of reaching his partner in this mood, Dell rapped his knuckles softly on the table and thought. Their job was to keep life in the herd until the lease went into effect—the first of March. A mighty big job, in itself. The hay, Calliope said, wouldn't last but a week, even skimping along as they'd been. After that——

"Boys," Tex broke eagerly into Dell's thoughts, "I ain't a deuce in the deck, when it comes to snow-ballin' a outfit through. But my pard, here, is high card. He's young, but he's winter wise. So, if you're honin' to slow up a little, an' ain't no objections——"

"Cripes, no!" the "boys" made haste to answer.

"Then, Dell, we'll elect you Curly Q foreman, pro tem!"

Dell's heart sang for joy. This was like the old

Tex—turning to him. But he wasn't at all sure he'd accept the election. He was proud they wanted him to. But it meant taking on his own shoulders all responsibility for the "starvation-demoralization-damnation" state of affairs. And he didn't want to be tied down now—with black trouble brewing, and Tex running wild. But some one had to do it——

They hoped *he* would—Tex, Dutch, and Calliope, watching him anxiously. As anxiously his gray eyes studied them, so vital to his success if he did take it up.

Old Dutch and Calliope might have been twins. Both were similarly stooped and spare. Even their old legs bowed the same. And their faded old eyes, the same pale blue, reflected the same light, honest and true. Their faces, the hue of old saddles, were stamped in the self-same pattern of seams. And more than skin-deep was the likeness, for they even *thought* the same. Their only outstanding difference was Calliope's predilection for untuneful song, and Dutch's conscientious objection to it.

Hector, with his touseled black head, his freckles that winter had tamed, but by no means subdued, was a regular boy. Violent in his likes and dislikes, loyal to a fault—if that can be—impulsive, impetuous, above all, mischievous, he was a young firebrand. He had been christened "Jefferson Hale," when too young to do anything about it. But, at a latter age, proceeded to make himself such a tease and torment—albeit, a lovable one—that he earned the nickname "Hector," and was inordinately proud of the more virile, "Heck."

Such were the men—for the boy, in his diminutive chaps, shirt, boots and bandanna, and manly courage, as proven by the way he'd raised the pitchfork in defense of his home, could not be excepted—who looked to Dell. Good men and true! He could ask for no better. They proved their mettle by being here. With Tex—worth any dozen of men—and for *June*—— Suddenly Dell had absolute faith in himself. He could move a mountain for June!

"Boys," he said, rising, "shake hands with your foreman! I'll do my best!"

CHAPTER V

HIS JOB!

NOW that he'd taken the reins, Dell was at a loss to proceed. His first act was to saddle a horse and make a tour of the Curly Q. Things seemed at an *impasse*. Riding down to the yards, he critically inspected the herd, huddled in ragged groups, its rough hair blowing up in the pitiless wind. And if it had seemed to him, at first sight, a nightmare, a delirium, it was now a hundredfold more so.

A glance at the hay confirmed Calliope's opinion that it would last but a week. And it was now three weeks before the first! Where was more coming from? Hale wouldn't have gone to Spokane for feed, if he could have bought it here. He'd mortgaged everything he possessed to raise that cash. And Dell wondered that he'd been able to, for a herd like this was a liability. Hay on Thunder River Range was precious as gold. And, at the prevailing price, every cow would eat her value in a month. At any rate, there was no time to ship now, for the need was immediate, imperative, and his chances to fill it—nil!

But, extending his survey far out to the white

range beyond, strangely enough, Dell found hope there. Decision marked his movements and he radiated hope, when he stamped into the kitchen, long after night fell.

When the weary crew had finished supper, the new foreman held them at the table and outlined a campaign of war—and this war was not to be with man, but with nature, inexorable, horrible.

"Boys," Dell said crisply, facing them on his feet, drawing inspiration from the proud confidence in his partner's eyes, "we can save the herd—or the bulk of it! But it means we've got to put up the fight of our lives. Here's my plan. Pull me up short, if I'm wrong. Then, if any of you can think of a better—shoot!"

Weary, worn out, as they were, even the old punchers jerked out of their slump, intent on that young face shining down with all the daring, high courage and vision of youth—vision, that keeps its eyes firmly fixed on the goal, nor sees the obstacles between.

"We've got to get some system to things—to organize. First, we'll cut up the herd in three bunches—steers, young cows, an' all of the strongest in one. This will be the main herd, an' I'll handle it. I'll drive it to range, an' make it rustle——"

"How?" availing himself of his prerogative, Dutch pulled him up short. "How you figger to make cows rustle their livin' in this snow, Dell?"

"With a scheme I seen worked in the Grand

Coulee," Dell enthusiastically outlined. "I knew one nester who pulled his whole herd through with it, in the hard winter of '98! Here it is: The hills are alive with range horses. I counted more than a hundred on my ride. They're tough, an' you can't kill 'em. We'll round up a bunch, an' hold 'em on the south slopes, where the grass is good under the snow.

"You-all know how a range horse paws snow, high, wide, an' handsome, eatin' what grass he can get at handy, an' then keeps travelin' on to double back over the same ground, when the sun gits to the pawed-up places an' bares a little more grass. Well, I'm goin' to keep the horses movin' right along, an' let the cows git second pickin's! A few mouthfuls of bunch grass a day, will keep life in a cow. An' with the brush an' moss they'll pick up, they'll live—three weeks!

"The second bunch"—Dell was creating confidence, and it added to his own—"will be made up of cows too weak to buck snow, but can rough it a bit. I'm turnin' 'em over to you, Dutch, an' Cal. Hold 'em down in the river bottom an' cut brush an' willow shoots like your life depended on it. They'll live a long time on that—I've seen it tried! You can change their diet an' help out a little by gatherin' an occasional sled load of moss from them tamarack groves over west of us. Moss ain't much for feed, but it'll help out in a pinch, an' that's sure what we're in!"

Now Dell looked at Tex, and there was in his gray eyes, as in Tex's dark ones looking back at him, all the strange and unusual affection they held for each other.

"The third lot will be weaklin's, down cows, an' calves. They git what hay's left. By careful feeding, it will hold out for them. That's your job, Tex. It's the hardest, but"—Dell grinned sympathetically—"you'll raise such a sweat liftin' them cows, you can't held but keep warm!"

"No; I'm swappin' with you, pard." Suddenly Tex was on his feet, too. "You take the down cows, I'll range the main herd. That's my job, Dell!"

Caught by the purposeful ring of his voice, Dell looked at him sharply. Tex's face was shadowed by more than the sleepless night, the fatigue of the day. And again Dell knew that lonely sensation of being in the dark, far from Tex, and a stranger to him.

"I'd—I'd rather not, Tex," he said slowly. "It means spendin' all day in the saddle, an' half the night. I don't mind it a bit, but—you'd freeze doin' it, Tex."

Again, with that haunting inflection, "That's my job!" said Tex, and the hungry longing Dell had seen in the depot, looked out of his eyes.

In the end, Dell gave in, thinking Tex considered it the dangerous job because of the hostile Box Bar men, but regretting his consent, as Tex gave his real reason:

"We've got to use every bit of strength them cows have left! I'll use hosses, like Dell says, to paw for the cattle an' break the trail, but—I'm rangin' them cows *straight to Thunder Brakes!* I'll have 'em right on the line, ready to move over the minit that lease takes effect!"

Heck's wild war whoop would have done honor to a Sioux brave. Even the old fellows flamed to his daring. But Dell's heart was heavy.

"Suppose you git the herd out there, an' Hale don't come back by the first," he cried anxiously. "What then, Tex?"

"I'm puttin' the herd on Thunder Brakes the first day of March," answered his partner with quiet force, "whether or not, Jeff Hale gits back!"

With one big fight on his hands, Dell couldn't worry too much about that.

And it was a fight—the battle they put up for the Curly Q! One that left scars on the soul of every man engaged in it. A fight with famine, misery, and killing cold. Not once—except at midday—did the temperature rise above zero. Nights, it dropped many degrees below. Warmth, comfort, rest—what were they? The men forgot they ever knew.

But some semblance of order was brought out of chaos. Hope infused the whole outfit. Calliope vowed that even the herd picked up.

Every hour of daylight Thunder River Valley resounded with the sharp ring of axes and Calliope's martial music, as the two old veterans slashed out the young willows and cottonwoods for the bellowing cattle, who had learned to follow the ring of the ax. And the cows greedily ate the tender shoots that were last year's growth, even gnawing down tough boughs to the thickness of an inch. They as greedily accepted the tamarack moss hauled in by sled, "while they rested," as Calliope said.

Every hour of daylight, and many of dark, Dell worked with the weaklings. He worked desperately to keep them on their feet, and lift to their feet those already down. To enable him to do this alone, he rigged up a set of blocks on a frame and hauled it from place to place. With a careful and scientific hand he doled out the precious remnant of hay. He worked alone, to the lonely, monotonous, nerve-racking bawls of the herd.

Out on the frozen range, daily farther from the comforts he craved, daily nearer the west fence of Thunder Brakes that was the dead line, rode Tex. He was mounted on the strongest Curly Q horse, for all day it must wallow belly-deep in snow, as Tex concentrated on the south slopes with the great herd of range horses they'd rounded up.

Heartbreaking work to hold them there, that in their own search for food, they might paw up great areas of snow for the bulk of the Curly Q herd trailing after! Heartbreaking work to keep the herd moving. For the cows, always adverse to traveling in snow, would almost have preferred to stand and freeze. But Tex made them rustle.

Ravenously, they cleaned up every spear of grass, every leafless whip of vine-maple, every vestige of brush in their path. Eating a black, broad trail, leading back to the Curly Q Ranch. And ahead—over the unbroken white ridges—Thunder Brakes!

So two weeks passed, and no word came from Hale. There was omnious quiet on the part of the Box Bar. Lying in his bunk beside Tex, too tired to sleep, his body one throb, one ache, Dell wondered why men worked like that. He knew why *he* did. But why did the rest? Not for money—there wasn't enough in the world to pay for it. Not for Jeff Hale——

"Wonder what kind of a hombre our boss is," he said aloud, on the chance that Tex was awake. "Readin' between the lines Dutch an' Cal drop, he ain't no saint, Tex. He fenced Cayuse Springs against Kinney, an', from what I catch, that started the fuss."

"He's far from a saint!" Tex's vehemence startled Dell. "You can bet your bottom dollar he deserves all he's gittin'! But we ain't killin' ourselves for Jeff Hale. We're fightin' for June—an' she's worth the best fight of any man's life!"

Again that sharp pang tore through Dell Young,

and he had to hold hard to Tex's promise, that—surer than any sure thing in the world—she wasn't the rock on which they'd split.

To Dell, the memory of June did not grow dim. It grew, instead, into the composite picture of all that was lovely, good, and true. He had only to shut his eyes to see her—as vivid, as glorious—still appealing to him. He even remembered the tiny dimple at the corner of her mouth. It must deepen, he thought, when she smiled. He longed unaccountably to see June Hale smile.

It didn't seem strange that he had loved her on sight. Love came to some men suddenly, like that. He had a bunkie once, who fell in love with a picture. And he'd heard of a man who went plumb loco over a stature he'd made himself. He had more reason than any of them. For when a hombre went along all his life, building up a picture of a girl—of all the things he loved in a girl—and along came that girl, *his* girl to the very last detail, it didn't take time to love her, for he already did!

Here in her home, working for her, with something at every turn to remind him of her, with stories of her constantly on the old punchers' tongues, he grew to know her as he would have been long knowing her had she been there.

Drearily, the wind might moan, and the cold bite deep, but June was in his heart. And his heart marked time till she came home.

They all marked time—until March first! Then would come the grand battle, short and sweet! For, whatever its outcome, it meant for the Curly Q punchers rest—rest——

"Two weeks," grimly Tex tolled off one night, "an' then—the *fireworks!*"

CHAPTER VI

JEFF HALE RETURNS

THAT winter! It made cold history in the great Northwest. It was a winter of tremendous loss, when the cattle industry of the Okanogan ranges was crippled, and the sacrifices men made to save their property were almost past belief. A winter when the poor nester, with but one cow or two, fed even the straw from the tick he slept on.

The big cattleman, unprepared for the unusual severity of it, saw his riches swept away, and himself placed on a par with the nester. Thousands upon thousands of cattle died on the range, and the green grass of a spring that had come too late to save them, sprang up to sunshine through their bleaching skulls. That winter the song of the coyote was never stilled and was hideous even to those who had loved it, for the high note of exultance in it that marked it as a feasting song.

Every heart prayed for an early Chinook—that dry, warm wind which comes out of the south, and takes the snow as if by magic. Every eye watched the southern skies for the black clouds that presaged it. They watched the weighted evergreens on the north slopes, that would slip their burden and spring erect at the first breath of it. They listened for the air to be filled with the curious little rushing sound they made—mellow, musical voice of the spring Chinook.

All along the valley, winter-weary Indians made medicine to haste its coming, and wore themselves out in the frenzied gyrations of the Chinook dance.

But it would come to late to save the Curly Q. And the reënforced crew battled on like demons, heroes—*men!*

Day after day, Tex was up before dawn and out in subzero weather, toiling at work that would have broken the spirit of most men. All day in the saddle, blue to the lips with cold, cussing, shivering, pulling cows out of the drifts with a frozen rope, forcing them, inch by inch, nearer the disputed lane.

His job! Why? Why, of all men, should Tex Rankin, whose blood was tempered to southern climes, choose it? Fiercely insist upon it? Suffer the tortures of the damned to do it!

None dreamed the agonies he suffered—none but Dell. And pride of him leaped high.

"You're a good soldier, Tex," he said huskily, riding out there one bitter, blue-gray day. "You couldn't put up a gamer fight, if them cows was your own!"

Tex looked at him out of a sunken face and dark-ringed eyes.

"If them was my cows," he gritted, "I'd let 'em

die peaceful! I'd curl up my toes, an' lie down in a drift along with them!"

Then why was he doing it? For June, he'd said!

"They say freezin's a easy death, Dell," Tex half moaned. "But they're as far from the truth, as that ticket agent's idea of hell!"

Suddenly Dell was alarmed. Tex looked sick. "If it gits too bad, Tex, you can quit."

"I ain't a quitter," Tex said sullenly, "I'm the world's—prize—fool!"

Not until long, long after did Dell understand the bitter self-mockery in that cry. But it rang in his ears as he ran his eye over the herd, scattered about in the cold sunshine. It was losing flesh rapidly, and there was a week till the first. Gravely, he turned back to his partner.

"Think you can hold out, Tex?"

Tex's jaw set at a stubborn angle. "They've *got* to! I ain't goin' through this, an' be licked in the end!"

In deepening alarm, Dell said earnestly, "Listen, Tex: We ain't heard a word from Hale. Till we do, we'd better stay on our side of the high-board fence. We ain't no right to——"

His partner's gesture of sharp impatience cut him short.

"Oh, well"—Dell put the best face on it he could—"mebbe I'm makin' a mountain out of a molehill. We ain't seen hide or hair of the Box Bar outfit since we come. Likely Kinney's threat was all blah!"

Tex smiled dryly. "You got another guess comin'," he said, swinging his horse about. "Follow my smoke, an' I'll show you, Dell!"

Wonderingly, Dell followed Tex up the long, forested slope ahead, to a high summit, where Tex stopped and, turning in the saddle, threw a long arm out toward the flats far below.

"Dell, that's Thunder Brakes!"

His blood quickening, his eyes lighting with interest, Dell looked down at the series of steplike mesas, terracing up from Little Klootch Creek, to a wild jumble of canyons and mountains; black, jagged chasms and cloud-piercing buttes. A fine place for an outlaw to play hide-and-seek in, Dell couldn't help thinking, if he had the law on his trail.

But the wind-swept flats were what held his interest. Treeless they were, and free from snow, showing tawny in sharp contrast to the dead white that bound them on every side. And the tawny color was bunch grass, thick and rank, with here and there, in sinklike depressions, patches of deeper brown, denoting where the rye grass grew, "acre wide and man high." Thunder Brakes—the promised land for the Curly Q herd!

"What do you see, Dell?" Tex asked impatiently. "No, down here! At the foot of this hill!"

What did Dell see? The west fence of Thunder

Brakes, white on the outside, where the hill protected it from the scouring wind, but brown on the other—and on the other side, dark riders! *Rush Kinney's men on fence patrol!*

"The ol' buzzard's watchin'!" Tex said grimly. "Every day since I started the herd, a rider on a black hoss has popped up on the sky line to chalk off my distance!"

"Bat Rouge!" Dell's eyes swung to Tex, black with emotion. "Remember, Tex, that night in Blue Buttes—he was ridin' a black!"

Tex nodded. "Dell, does it look like a fight?"

"But we——" Dell began helplessly.

But Tex cut in, "Pard, there's a hot time comin', but it's *my* fight, savvy? With you to help me, I'll see it through!"

Cruelly depressed, Dell rode back to the Curly Q. Why did Tex exclude him like that? Hadn't he fought as hard as Tex? Wasn't it his fight, too? Hadn't he as much right as Tex to fight for June?

As he turned his horse up Thunder River to speak to the old punchers, Calliope's voice came to meet him, lifted in tired, but dauntless song:

> "Ha-ha-ha! You an' me,
> Li'le brown jug, don't I love thee!
> Ha-ha-ha!——"

"Har-har-har!" sarcastically roared Dutch. "Oh, *can't* you be still! Cal, you got my nerves plumb rasped raw! *Talk,* if you got any strength to waste on your jaw, but for the love of gooseberry marmalade, don't *sing!*"

And, as Dell imagined, in an effort to turn Calliope's vocal activities into pleasanter channels, he continued, "Why d'ja reckon June don't write?"

"Dunno," Cal replied, peeved.

"Think Jeff's hurt bad?"

"No news is good news, but I hope to heaven he's hurt so bad he don't git over it afore spring!"

Unconsciously, as Dutch dittoed that, Dell reined in his horse.

"Them boys is the best danged waddies I ever seen—bar none!" Cal declared fervently. "But when Jeff comes, they go! Won't make any difference to *him,* what they've done an' what he owes 'em! They'll go jist the same!"

"Cal," Dutch was much too engrossed to see Dell approaching, "did it ever strike you, Jeff's a mite off?"

"He sure is on *that* subject! I've often figgered he musta had something to make him that a way—some big trouble, that preyed on his mind."

"It's a cinch he brung it on hisself, if he did!" Dutch said warmly. "An' he's a-hatchin' hisself another batch of the same! For, Cal, he's sure takin' the wrong tack with June! Spirits is natural in a young thing. You can't keep 'em bottled. Leastwise, Cal, you can't keep 'em corked. They jist fizzle an' foam, till all of a sudden, off pops the lid! That li'le gal's been an angel to Jeff, but——" his jaws closed like a trap, as Dell coughed a warning.

But Dell had something else to worry him now. What particular treatment of June by her father did the old men resent? What mysterious connection did it have with him and Tex? He knew now how desperately he wanted to stay. To save the herd for June! To be the kind of a man she took him for—and keep things together for her, somehow!

He couldn't part with Dutch or Calliope, either. They were princes to work with. Never whimpered. Took their turns in the kitchen. Heck, too! Why, he almost ran his legs off on errands and chores! He liked Heck a lot, even if the kid didn't like him.

Heck didn't put salt in his coffee, or tacks in his boots, or set the mouse trap to catch his toes when he rolled from his bunk. He didn't even pay him the compliments of "cussing him out," as he did Dutch and Calliope when they displeased him. He just ignored him when he could, and was polite when he couldn't. And Dell was sorry for this.

Chancing to run across him down in the bottom once, stacking dead limbs for the heater "to warm Tex up," Dell asked him outright:

"Heck, what you got against me?"

The boy flushed and dug his toe in the snow. Then, looking up at Dell, came out with it manfully:

"You're *his* pal!"

Jealous of Tex! A wave of pity swept over Dell. "Why can't we all three be pals?" he suggested.

Hector considered that for a moment. "A hombre can't pal with *two!*" he said candidly. "An' I like Tex best!"

For which Dell didn't blame him.

"Never knowed him to take a shine like that to but one man before," Cal told Dell as, together, they watched the boy riding off to the range with hot coffee for Tex. "That was Mojave, who worked here about two years ago. Come to think of it, he was a heap like your pard. Deep, I mean, an' devil-may-care. But folks said Mojave was a bad actor before he come here."

"Where is he now?"

"Workin' for the Box Bar, dang him!"

If they had trouble then, Dell thought pityingly, it was going to make it tragic for Heck—fighting a former pal.

He liked to watch Tex and the boy together. Sometimes of an evening, when the big fellow was safe inside, and for the moment, the day's trials were crowded out, Dell would hear the boy describing to Tex, to the last gory detail, the battle to come. Always the Curly Q was victorious. Always he concluded with Bat Rouge squirming under his hero's heel.

"Gee!" he'd cry rapturously, "I can't wait, Tex, to see you an' Bat mix!"

Often, Dell would hear Tex telling the boy stories of Texas, especially the stirring tale of the Alamo. Over and over, Hector must hear it. He never tired of it. And he learned to swear by Sam Houston, too. And, sometimes, when Tex was most discouraged, most used up by cold and fatigue, the boy's clear voice would rise in the old battle cry of the Texans: "Remember the Alamo!"

It never failed to rouse Tex. And to the boy, he poured out his homesick yearning, now all but unbearable. He pictured to him the hot plains of Texas, where lizards and snakes "skally-hooted" everywhere. The "forests" of prickly pear on the Neuces, in which many a rider, lost, had been "crucified" on the cruel spines they bore.

"The boy's eyes would glisten.

"I'm goin' there, Tex!" Dell heard him announce one night. "I'll go back with you."

"When you grow up, Heck," qualified Tex in his slow drawl, "an' your dad gives you leave."

"He won't ever let me!" flashed the boy bitterly. "He never lets me have any fun. But I'll go anyhow—I'll run off an' go! You'll take me, Tex?"

"You'd leave June?"

The boy's face fell at the implied reproach, then cleared at a simple decision, "We'll take June! It's a go, Tex!"

Dell seemed to smother up all at once, and walked out in the night. Stars studded the sky like diamonds, shedding their million facets of light. The cows lowed hunger. A coyote howled to the frozen moon. Somewhere, out there, dying by inches, was the main bulk of the Curly Q herd. Somewhere, out there, men guarded the range that would save it. And, here—Tex and he—where were they drifting?

Next day, a neighboring rancher, returning from Blue Buttes, delivered a letter from June. She was bringing her father home on the noon train, and wanted the sled sent to meet them. Calliope, who could best be spared at the time, went in.

Just before dusk Dell heard them coming. Forgetting everything but June's home-coming, he released the calf he was tending, and straightened to look. Eagerly his eyes leaped over old Cal on the front seat, over the bundled form of a man in the rear, to the little blue-cloaked figure beside him. Eagerly, his lips and eyes smiled in certain expectancy of some greeting.

But no one even looked toward him. And, with dozens of bawling cows around him—was his not unreasonable thought—he was a mighty hard person to overlook.

Anxiously his eyes pierced the distance to June. Her face was set straight ahead, white and unhappy. A strange chill, strange dread, fell upon Dell. When Hale came, they'd go, every one had said! But he couldn't believe it. His spirits refused to be damped. He'd see June at supper. He counted the moments till then.

But long before then, Calliope rode off to the range, returning in an hour or so with Tex.

"Dell"—the old puncher was the picture of woe—"I wisht I was a hundred miles from this ranch! But I ain't—an' he made me the goat!" He looked long at the stricken cowboy, with wet, old eyes, then tragically blurted, "The boss wants to see you!"

Dell forced a smile to his lips. "It's natural, he'd want to," he replied, but his lightness was forced.

"It's a howlin' crime!" vowed Cal.

Walking with Tex to the house, Dell was too upset to pay any heed to his partner. But, at the door, the big puncher stayed his hand on the knob with a cry, so hoarse, so strained, that he'd never in the world have known it was Tex's voice:

"Wait, pard! Wait till I git a grip on myself!"

Dell saw that Tex was shaking like a leaf and white to the lips. But whatever emotion possessed him, it passed in a moment, and he was again his still, cool self.

Then they went in.

CHAPTER VII

THE PLEDGE

THEY passed through the kitchen without seeing any one. But when they would have entered the living room, Heck burst out of it and flung himself upon Tex and clung to him, sobbing as though he would never let go. And while his partner strove to quiet the boy, Dell, chilled by this portent, walked into the room.

June was standing by the table, under the light of the chandelier. No snow, now, on her blue dress, bright curls, or long lashes. But there was snow in her cheeks, and she seemed frozen there. She was still the girl of the storm.

Jeff Hale, half sat, half reclined, in the deep morris chair. His position, alone, indicated his hurt. Nor did he change it, save to nod briefly as Dell came in.

He was tall—tall as Tex, Dell imagined. And a man you had only to see once, to never forget. For his hair was snow white, sweeping back from a brow, high and white, though the rest of his narrow, long face was bronzed. His deep-set eyes were the blackest, most piercing, Dell had ever seen in the head of a man. He had a thin, high-bridged nose. His lips, too, were thin, and saturnine in expression, and the true index to his character.

"Hard as nails," was Dell's swift summing up of him, as Tex came in, leading the still sobbing boy by the hand.

"Boys"—Jeff Hale's impersonal stare held them both, and his voice was as hard as Dell's first impression of him—"I'm thankin' you for what you've done for the Curly Q. An' I'm askin' you to take this money in payment, an' go!"

Many predictions had not prepared Dell for this flat dismissal. Amazed, he looked up from the bills in Hale's long fingers, into his deep, inscrutable eyes. But Dell wasn't seeing Hale. He was seeing Tex—out there on the range, blue to the lips, suffering, game! In payment—*that?* For what Tex had done! Dell's blood boiled.

"Got any reason?" his voice rang out loudly on the dead hush of the room.

"If I have," Hale said coldly, "it's my own."

"If you have," Dell cried hotly, "be man enough to kick through with it! We've worked like dogs here. We've got a right to know why we're treated like dogs. Why, man, you *can't* let us go! Think of the fix you'd be in—the fix you *are* in!"

"That's my business, too!" Hale flared wrathfully. "Git off the place—*pronto!* I've fired you both!"

It was Jeff Hale's ranch. So, as far as Dell was concerned, that settled the matter. With a last look at the pale little ghost that was June, he was turning to go, when Tex thrust the boy from him, and walked right up to Hale.

"It's no go!" Tex said coldly, his haggard face set. "When we met your girl at the depot an' heard the shape things was in, we ditched our own plans to help her out. We couldn't stand by an' see her ruined. An' we sure won't now, when we can catch a glimmer of daylight ahead. We've worked like dogs, as my pard says, but we won't take our time, an' pull out like whipped pups! Not on your daguerreotype! You didn't hire us, Hale, an' you can't fire us!"

The sheer nerve of that speech stunned all but Hale. He jerked up in his chair, seemed on the point of violent outburst, when he got a grip on himself. Even relaxed, as if he found something to his liking in this.

"If you'd rather take your dismissal from her," he said, with slow insolence, "I'm agreeable." And, with the air of one certain of obedience here, he commanded the girl: "Fire them, June!"

To his utter amazement, she defied him.

"I won't!" and her eyes weren't blue, but black, in her mutiny. "Dad, you can't make me! It means losing everything. They were good enough to come when we most needed them. We need them no less now. I won't tell them to go! I'm thanking them with my whole heart for even wanting to stay!"

Brave in her first rebellion, she faced his wrath with unflinching eyes. And he turned from her in a passion.

"Git out!" he roared at the cowboys. "Or I'll show you who's boss of this ranch!"

"That's easy to see!" drawled Tex, his insolence a dead match for Hale's, and before which the rancher was helpless to do more than sputter and fume. "Sure, you rule the roost! You're the Great-I-Am! That ain't all you are, Jeff Hale—you're selfish as sin! You're sinkin' fast, an' you don't give two whoops who you drag down with you!"

That this was a queer way to go about getting a job, wasn't what startled Dell. It was another, more startling change in Tex. He'd thought he knew Tex pretty well, but he didn't know him at all. When Tex got mad, he got cold. He wasn't cold now, but he sure was mad!

"Who suffers most, if you lose this ranch?" Tex blazed down at Hale. "You? Not on your life! You've lived your life, an' you ain't made a splash in a hog wallow! You don't care that this boy an' girl, here—who can't help it, if you're their dad—lose *their* start in life! You don't give a tinker's dang! You're mortgaged to the hilt. If you lose your herd, they lose their home! There's a chance—

a slim one—of pullin' out now, if we stay on. But for some fool reason that won't bear mentionin' you'd fire us an' kill their only chance! You'd even beggar this girl——"

Dell thought Jeff Hale would have a fit then and there.

"June," he panted, his eyes rolling wildly, "git me a gun!"

She gave no sign of hearing, and helplessly Hale sank back, grinding in baffled fury:

"You're mighty concerned about *her!*"

"Somebody has to be," retorted the Texan, "if her own father ain't!"

That speech seemed to loosen a devil in Tex, for his throat set up a visible throbbing, and he appeared to tower a mile above Hale.

"Father?" he mocked, and not even Dell guessed how wildly his heart beat then, or the pang that tore quiveringly through his breast. "What kind of a father are you? Even an animal looks out for its young—fights for it—gives it the best it can provide! But you——"

June's hands went protestingly out to Tex, but he gave her no heed.

"You're the kind of a father that would walk out on a kid, an' not be concerned if it died or lived——"

"Don't!" Hale's face was bloodless, and he cowered from Tex.

"Why not?" Tex mocked him relentlessly. "Why not hear the truth for once? You're the kind of a father that could tear a kid from its moth——"

"For heaven's sake!" Hale screamed. Wildly he looked about, as though for some way of escape. Then his eyes fell on his daughter.

"June," he whispered thickly, "leave the room!"

Wordlessly, she obeyed him. Forgotten by all, Hector slipped behind Tex. A painful silence fell over all. In it, Jeff Hale slowly fought back to composure, all the while staring at Tex like a man hypnotized.

Like he'd been beaten, Dell thought, for the first time in his life, and had a holy fear and respect for the man who had done it. But there was more in his look. Guilt? Remorse? Dell couldn't decide. As for Tex—the last ounce of fight had gone out of him.

"Why do you want this job?" Hale demanded suspiciously, at last. "Most men would shy a mile off from it! What makes you so crazy to work for me?"

"To finish what I've started"—Tex said simply—"to save the Curly Q herd."

There was a breathless moment, in which Hale seemed to be weighing his words, weighing the two men, and to arrive at some hard decision.

"Young man," he told Tex, more calmly than he'd spoken yet, "you've said things to me to-night that

I never thought a man could say—an' live! More than *you'd* have said, if I hadn't been helpless! But your words go deeper than you know—though some of 'em are beyond me. For fear that other folks think as you do—that I'm unmindful of June an' the boy—I'll keep you till spring—on one condition!" Again he embraced both in his terrible scrutiny.

"What?" asked Tex, in a wilted tone.

"That you'll give me your word of honor," hoarsely stipulated Jeff Hale, "to speak no word of love to my daughter!"

Both cowboys were outraged.

"You—you'd even insult her!" Tex blazed up again.

The rancher lifted his hand.

"I don't mean it like that. Nor I ain't explainin' to you what I do mean—more than this: I've lost a lot in my lifetime. June's all I got left. She's mine, an' I'm goin' to keep her. I'd rather see her dead, than married to the best man on earth! An' I'll see the man dead before he gits her! If you're honest in wantin' the job——"

"I'll meet that condition," Tex silenced him. "I give you my word!"

"An' you?" Hale's piercing eyes bent upon Dell.

Dell's heart beat madly. Not to speak of love to June! Could he promise that? But he had no choice. To refuse meant to leave her forever. If he agreed, he'd be with her till spring.

"I swear!" he solemnly promised.

"All right!" Hale breathed more freely then. "But I'm warnin' you both, it won't be healthy to go back on that pledge! You're here to work. You go when the herd's pulled through. That's understood! An' I want you to savvy this, too: What I say, I mean; an' what I say goes! I won't be argued with. An' I'll never take ag'in, what I took to-night! Now, let's git down to cases."

Dell didn't enter much into the discussion that followed. He was finding out what "sort of a hombre" Hale was at last, and was dazed by his finding. Calliope had told Hale just what they had done, and he approved of it it grudgingly. But he came mighty near praising Tex when told that the main herd was within two miles of Thunder Brakes.

"Then you're goin' on?" Tex asked eagerly.

"I am!" Hale's jaw set like a rock. "I've got a lease on that place, an' I'd like to see Rush Kinney stop me! The Box Bar's three to our one, but right is might!"

Seeing that the interview was nearing an end, Dell reminded him, "You ain't told us yet how you got hurt."

That threw Hale into a fury again. "Some coward slugged, manhandled an' robbed me!" he raged. "Waylaid me in the dark, on my way to the hotel. When I woke up in the hospital, I found I'd been robbed of every cent I'd rustled in the hope of buyin' hay!"

"Think the Box Bar was back of it?" queried Tex tensely.

They were taken aback by the positiveness with which Hale denied the suspicion. "No, that's *one* thing they ain't guilty of! It was a sailor."

Astounded by that, they both beseiged him. How did he know that? Spokane wasn't a seaport! What would a sailor be doing four hundred miles from a boat? Bat Rouge had taken a train ride about that time. They could find out where, if Hale said so. Might it not have been Bat? Did he see his assailant?"

"No! It was dark, I told you," Hale said stubbornly. "But it wasn't Bat—it was a sailor."

He gave no reason for that strange and groundless belief. And, later, coming to know him better, they'd have known better than to expect him to. For, as Calliope said, "If Jeff gits a thing in his head, all creation can't pry it out with a pickax. Jeff's one part pure cussedness, an' three parts mule! We shipped a boatload of steers once, down the Okanogan to Portland, an' Jeff had a run-in with the deck hands over the loadin'. Ever since then, a man couldn't pull off a crime on the Great Sahara, but he'd swear it was a sailor!"

Still sticking to that belief now, Hale instructed them:

"Go on as you're doin'. Crowd the cows right up to Thunder Brakes! Kinney won't dare bother them on government range, an' we'll all be on hand to put them on it Monday!"

Jubilant at the way things had turned out, the boys were hurrying through the kitchen to stun old Cal and Dutch with the news, when June came running to meet them.

"Good-by!" she cried, tears in her eyes and voice. "Please believe there's one Hale that's grateful!"

"Good-by?" echoed Tex gently. "Girl, you're always sayin' good-by. But you ain't rid of us by a long shot. We're goin' to stay!"

She stared at him blankly, unable to believe.

"That's on the level, June," Tex smiled deep into her tear-starred eyes.

"How"—she was tremulous with wonder and joy—"whatever did you say to dad, that he let you stay?"

"Oh, Jiminy, what *didn't* he say!" whooped Heck, all doubled up in a spasm of glee. "He said he wouldn't make love to you!"

The girl's distress was painful to Dell, though he'd never seen anything half so pretty as June was then—all colored up pink.

"Dad can't know how he humiliates me," loyally she made excuse for Hale. "He—he wouldn't do that, if he did. I don't care—for myself. But I hate it for you. It—it's ridiculous! As if a man couldn't come on the place without wanting to make love to me!"

A far from ridiculous supposition, Dell thought. Then he was pink and panicky, too, as Heck, from a safe distance, made everything definite.

"Sis, Dell promised, too!"

Flaming many shades pinker, June ran from the room.

"You young limb of Satan!" Dell made a wild grab for the boy, but Heck slipped through his hands like an eel, and ran to Tex for protection. Not that Tex was able to give him any, for he was helpless with laughter, himself.

Such was the price Dell Young and his partner, Tex Rankin, paid for their jobs on the Curly Q. Not to love June? No! Not to *speak* love! To that they were pledged. But no pledge ever invented by man can be laid upon eyes. Eyes speak love as truly as lips, and volumes of love can be put in a glance. But could romance possibly blossom in such an atmosphere of misery, cold and strife? It could! And be the more deeply rooted, more exquisitely hued for its cruel struggle for life.

The cold, toilsome days passed like a nightmare. Each took more out of the crew than sleep could restore. Often the partners fell into their bunk, too weary to do more in the way of undressing than pull off their boots. Each day found the crisis nearer. And at last the Curly Q herd was in sight of the promised land!

Down by the river, the two old punchers faithfully slaughtered the brush. Calliope still sang as he worked, but the text of his song was as bad as his faint and quavery tone.

"The stream's a-runnin' jist the same,
The willers on each side,
Are bendin' o'er the grave of Rosie Lee——"

Such was the tenor of his songs now. Sometimes he'd entreat the world in general to, "Toll the bell, for li'le Nell," or, more appropriately to, "Play the fife slowly, an' beat the drum lowly, an' play the Dead March," as they bore him along. And he dragged each of these pitiful wails out to the bitter end. For Dutch was much too fagged to protest.

"Reckon nothin' will ever surprise me ag'in," Cal vowed once in a breathing spell, "after Jeff's keepin' the boys on!"

"Nor me!" Dutch agreed.

Calliope dug deep in his pocket. "Toss you two bits, Dutch, to see which June picks."

"It ain't worth the effort," Dutch sighed, leaning hard on his ax. "She could shut her eyes, an' pick. Either one, she'd git a *man!*"

After another back-breaking seige, he asked Cal what day it was. The days had run right into each other, till he'd lost all track of time.

"February twenty-sixth," Cal spoke up promptly.

"Three days more, an' we'll swap these axes for guns!"

They whacked away another while in silence.

"Dutch," Cal said solemnly, "them Lone Star waddies sure believe in bein' prepared. Tex never leaves the bunk house without lookin' over his big six-gun. An' this mornin' I saw him dig out that ol' saddle scabbard an' take along the .30-30!"

CHAPTER VIII

LIGHTER MOMENTS

STEADILY the ominous date crept up. How ominous, Tex could realize best. For he was working now in sight of the Box Bar men. And he had almost hourly evidence of Rush Kinney's determination to prevent Jeff Hale from making the one move that could forestall ruin.

The men at the Curly Q looked forward to March first, as to a release. For, once Thunder Brakes was open to them, Dutch and Cal would be liberated from the slavish slashing down there, and, having driven the cows in their care slowly over the trail beaten by the main herd, be free to help Dell. For Dell's cows couldn't be moved. On the short rations, to which he'd been forced to reduce them, they had not even been able to hold their own. He hated to think how many they'd already dragged over the hill. The hay was practically gone. But they planned to cut rye grass on Thunder Brakes, and haul it down to them.

Nothing was said of the coming fight for possession of Thunder Brakes. Just how Hale meant to wrest it from the Box Bar—well-manned, fresh, and as determined to keep him off, as he was to go on—

his crew was naturally anxious to know. But he didn't divulge his plans. And they all knew better than to ask, or make any suggestions. He was still too weak to get outside, and they rarely saw him except at meals.

"I'm worried about him," June confided to Dell at the feed yards one day. "He acts so queer—not a bit like himself. He just sets for hours, and stares into space. And to-day I ran across him up in the attic. He had taken mother's picture out of the trunk, and was crying over it. He never would look at that picture before—or even let me."

"Your mother's dead?" Dell had heard that, but he wanted to keep her talking to him.

"She died when I was little——" As if, Dell grinned, she was ever anything else! "I don't remember her much. Dad won't talk of her. Won't talk of his life before he came here. We came from Texas—that's all I know. And I've quit asking him about mother. He loved her so much, he can't bear to hear her mentioned, I guess. Hector's my half-brother. Dad married again. My stepmother died after we came here."

Dell was seeing a lot of June these days. Spring calves were coming. And, due to the general weakened condition of the mothers, they had to have exceptional care. With the crew overworked as it was, his task fell on June and the boy. They had a nursery out in the barn, to which Tex often brought in a bawling, long-legged little addition across his saddle.

Naturally, Dell working right handy there, was often called in to help June with an obstreperous calf that just wouldn't keep its feet out of the bucket, and they'd laugh at its antics. Naturally, too, their hands often met in the plain course of duty, and Dell couldn't help tingling clear to his toes, pledge or no pledge. Once, when June's hands were so cold that the pain made her half sick, Dell told her nothing took the frost out so quickly as to run them through somebody's hair. It was easier for him to take his hat off than for her to do so, so he did, and she did, standing so close to him to do it that her blue eyes laughed right into his! She told him, she liked straight, dark hair like his, and he said he didn't. He liked short, brown curls all crowded down by a red tam-o'-shanter, and all pushed up by the big collar of a fuzzy red sweater. Then they both laughed, and her hands *did* get warm.

Sometimes, of course, she had to work in the house. But it never was long till he went in, too. And there she'd be, pouring his coffee, or flitting around with a hot dish in her hand. No matter how tired or busy he was—and he sure was plenty of both—it was no trouble to fetch her a bucket of water, or split up some wood. And Dell didn't give two shucks when he heard Heck telling Tex that he was a "mush"!

He could hardly wait until spring. Then he and Tex would be fired, and released from that pledge. Then he could tell June just how he felt. But it was more wintry than ever—as if all the cold since last fall had piled up for now.

So Dell and June—without "soldiering" any, either of them—had long talks of her life on the ranch. Reading between the lines again, Dell got as mad as a hornet at how her father had tried to "bottle young spirits," which even old Calliope knew couldn't be done.

It wasn't in any wave of self-pity that June told him either, but just to talk to somebody young enough to get her viewpoint. It was something she hadn't had much chance of doing before. For Jeff Hale had been awfully strict with her since she was grown. Wouldn't even let her have any girl friends. But during all her kid days, Janice Kinney and she had been great friends.

"Any relation to the Box Bar Kinney?" Dell asked.

"His daughter." June couldn't imagine why Dell looked so dumb.

"I can't feature him bein' a daddy!" the cowboy confessed. "Somehow, I had him pictured a blood-curdlin' big ogre who eats little girls!"

They both laughed again.

"He's not!" June was honestly sweet, and sweetly honest. "You'd likely think him a nice, old man. I always thought so till he burned our hay. And," her eyes were suddenly wistful, "I still think Janice is the nicest girl on this range."

Of course, Dell took an exception to that.

"Oh, wait till you see her!" June blushed a little. "She's pretty, and as good as she's pretty. Full of the dickens, too! We had lots of fun. But I haven't seen her to speak to for three years now. Dell, there's a reason! The last time she came over—Bat was working here then——"

"Bat worked *here*—on the Curly Q!" Dell couldn't credit his ears.

"Why, didn't you know that? He was our foreman. He was"—Dell was entranced by her girlish giggle—"he was the last man under sixty that dad ever hired!"

"Then *that's* why every one said we'd go!" Dell saw the light at last. "Because we were young!"

She nodded. "You see, dad's so settled and serious he doesn't like young folks around, or for me to go with young folks—or have young times."

Settled and serious, *nothing,* was Dell's savage thought. Selfish and mean, was what he was! Had been married twice himself, the old sinner, and wouldn't let June even get married once!

"But to go on with my story—of why Janice quit coming: Bat, he—took a fancy to me. And I—well, I thought he was pretty nice, too. You see," she put in, by way of apology, "I wasn't but sixteen then, and had no very high ideals of men."

"Well, Janice came over one night, and wanted me to go to the big dance the stockmen were giving up at the schoolhouse. Bat offered to take us. But dad's dead set against dancing, so I knew it would be useless to ask. Heavens, how I wanted to go! I've never wanted anything half so bad in my life. I'd learned to dance with a phonograph over at Janice's, and I was crazy about it. Still am, for that matter! Besides, I had a new dress—a ruffly, white muslin, with a pink-ribbon sash. And all the time Janice kept talking, I kept seeing myself in *that* dress at *that* dance, till—— Guess what I did?"

Dell couldn't guess.

"Sneaked out, like a thief in the night, as the books say, and went with Janice and Bat. Wasn't that awful?"

"Perfectly terrible!" Dell was properly shocked.

She made an impudent face at him, which, had no pledge existed, he'd surely have kissed. "Well," she sighed deeply, "it wasn't half as terrible, as what came of it. For dad followed me there! I was the life of the party, if I do say so—and please let me say so," she pleaded pathetically, "for it was my first and last dance!"

No—not her last dance! But June couldn't know that!

"I was dancing with Bat, when dad came in. Oh, Dell, I could die of shame when I think of it! He yanked me right off the floor, then read the riot act to the crowd. Told them dancing was 'the devil's amusement,' called it 'hugging to music,' and things like that. He'd have killed Bat, but for the men grabbing his gun. He called him down something awful, and fired him. Then he started on Janice. Called her a 'minx' and a 'hussy,' and forbid her even to speak to me!"

"That's what started the fuss, then?" Dell said slowly. "Cal told us it was a difference of opinion on what made up human sin."

The little tam-o'-shanter nodded agreement.

"Rush Kinney thinks as much of his daughter, as dad does of me. So he waltzed right over here, and told dad to start apologizing and to apologize hard! Dad was too stubborn, and anyhow he thought he was right. They quarreled, and, since then it's been awful. Somebody stampeded our cattle. Dad blamed Kinney. We *know* Bat had a hand in it. He went to work for the Box Bar when dad fired him. Then dad fenced in Cayuse Springs to get even, and Kinney swore he'd run dad out of the country. He's just about doing it, too!"

He was a long way from doing it, Dell said firmly, but he thought it would serve Hale right if he did.

A man ought to be shot for corralling a girl like June. She didn't kick either. The most she would own, was that it was lonesome—at times.

"Does Bat—fancy you still?" he asked the question that all this while had burned in his mind.

"Far from it!" the little dimple northwest of June's mouth deepened and danced. "I came to my senses right after the dance. Bat wanted me to meet him without dad's knowing it, and I added my opinion of him to dad's! You see, it was only a kid fancy with me. But talk about the fury of a *woman* scorned! A woman wouldn't be in it with Bat. He's hated me like poison ever since. Now, he's wild about Janice. He's ready to fight if another man looks at her. He *loves* to fight, and he's the best fighter in this country. So he keeps the other boys pretty well scared off."

"Now, that you're growed up, an' all," Dell asked tensely, as they moved toward the feed rack, steadying between them—oh, shades of romance!—a wabbly old cow, "jist what's your ideal of a man?"

June caught her breath at his earnestness. As if she'd tell *him!* Then twin imps danced in her eyes, and she did!

"A hard-working buckaroo about twenty-two, with gray eyes, dark hair, and a nick in his chin—— *No!*" in panic, as Dell made a dive for her. "Remember, you promised dad!"

Then as Dell halted, crushed with remorse at how near he'd come to breaking that pledge, the impact of a snowball took all the jaunty slant out of her tam, and she dashed off after Heck, running him down in a drift, and washing his face for him well.

Shucks! She was just teasing him, too! But Dell grinned happily as he went on with his work. Somehow, he felt guilty—having these sessions with June. It was as if he were taking an unfair advantage of Tex—Tex, out there on the range, freezing for her, dying a thousand deaths. For he'd known from the first that Tex loved June.

Still, Tex saw a lot of her, too. Almost every day she rode out to where he was. Dell wondered what June and Tex talked of. Serious stuff, he could tell that by their faces when they rode in. About Texas, maybe—June had said they came from there, too. But he wasn't worrying about Tex taking an unfair advantage of him. Tex wouldn't go back on a pledge. Dell would bank his life on it!

When spring came, he and Tex would settle this thing. But wasn't he taking a lot for granted? Likely June wouldn't have either of them on a bet! He couldn't see for the life of him, why she should love *him*. No girl could see him anyway, when Tex was around. But suppose she did. How could he be happy—even with June—if it meant a falling out with Tex?

He couldn't keep Tex out of his mind these days. He looked so bad—as if he'd been dragged through a knot hole and was keeping up on pure grit alone. Dell was glad the strain was most over. For this was the last day of February, and to-morrow—Thunder Brakes!

CHAPTER IX

A BROKEN PLEDGE

OUT there on the range, keeping up on pure grit this last and coldest day—zero at noon—Tex brought the herd within a quarter mile of the dead line. All day, across the silver snow, black against a clear turquoise sky, he saw Box Bar riders, like buzzards, watching his snailing approach. And along toward night, as Bat Rouge and another horseman halted at the fence, looking his way in what appeared to be earnest colloquy, Tex, obedient to a sudden impulse, rode over.

In Bat's eyes, as Tex's horse plowed up, was the same deadly challenge they'd held at Blue Buttes. But they fell before the driven intensity of Tex's look, and Bat resumed his contemptuous survey of the emaciated herd.

Swinging his horse broadside of the fence, Tex coolly joined in the survey.

"Not much for beef, are they?" he spoke with a mock friendliness which deceived neither of the men.

"Ought to git something out of their hides," commented Bat, in the same lying tone.

"Too much loss in that," Tex said evenly. "We aim to stuff them hides before we sell."

"Yeah?" Bat turned malevolent eyes on Tex. "With which—snowballs?"

"Not any more!" Tex assured him. "That bunch grass behind you will be stuffin' them hides this time to-morrow!"

"To-morrow! They were amazed by his frankness.

"That's what *you* think!" sneered Bat, recovering.

"That's when!" Tex said offhandedly. "You hombres sure done a lot of cold and unnecessary riding. My boss ain't no more right on Thunder Brakes, than yours has—till to-morrow! An' he's strong for what's right. To-morrow the lease goes in effect, an' to-morrow the herd goes on!"

It was too cold to sit long in the saddle, even with a fire burning within one, and Bat, a little in awe of this man's cool nerve, wheeled his horse.

"Hold on, Bat!" Tex called easily. "I got something of yours." And, as Bat suspiciously watched his action, he fished in his pocket, brought up the train check, and held it out. "Here, you dropped this in the stable that night."

A red flush darkened Bat's face, and his hand unconsciously extended, jerked back in fear.

"What you tryin' to do—frame me?" he shrilled.

Tex grinned mockingly. "You know the ol' sayin' about a guilty conscience, Bat!"

"It ain't mine!" Bat denied furiously, with something more potent than rage. "I never dropped it! I ain't been on a train in a year!"

Knowing that first was a lie, for he'd seen him drop it, Tex made a wild plunge. "These marks say the fellow who owned it was comin' up from Spokane three weeks ago!"

Goaded to reckless speech, by that taunting tone and grin, Bat jeered thickly, "Yeah—go on! Next you'll be sayin' it was me who robbed an' beat up Jeff Hale!"

"No," Tex said coolly, noting the amazement that shot through Bat's eyes, "you didn't do that. Hale said it was a sailor."

Strangely, that infuriated Kinney's foreman more. "I know your game!" he cried, with naked hate. "Hale hired you for this Thunder Brakes fracas! He had you sent up here! You—you Texas gunman! All right! Come on! I'll be loaded for you. Remember what you said—you'd make it worth my while!"

He spurred off like a man devil-possessed. But the other man with him lingered.

"Say, pard," he said apologetically, "how's the boy –Heck?"

Tex looked at him hard. He was a gnarled little man, with a pallid mustache, and a cold eye that fascinated Tex. He recognized the type. This must be Mojave—Hector's old pal—and a bad actor, he'd heard. Looking at him, Tex believed all he'd heard. He made a mental note of the fact, that, when the clash came, this quiet, inoffensive little fellow would be the dangerous one, and not Bat Rouge, for all his bluster and threat.

"How's Heck?" Tex echoed shortly. "I ain't heard him kickin' none."

Into the cold eyes crept a light curiously warm and wistful. "Reckon he hates me a lot."

Honesty compelled Tex to say, "Can't see that he does."

The man's face lighted with pleasure. "Say, I'm glad! I got to thinkin' a heap of the kid, an' he sure did of me. I stayed over there on his account as long as I could. But I couldn't git on with Hale. He's narrer as a boot lace, an' stiff-necked as all——"

"He's my boss," Tex cut in coldly.

"Sure," Mojave said understandingly. "An' Rush Kinney's mine! While I eat his salt, I fight his battles! Pard, I'll shore be slingin' lead at you to-morrow, but to-day I'm askin' a favor of you—tell Heck I'm sorry as sin things turned out this way!"

Tex remembered to do that, the minute he got back to the Curly Q.

"Gee," Heck said tearfully, "Mojave didn't need to tell *me!*"

Supper that last night was a sober affair, as well it might be. They were still in the dark as to Hale's intentions, so they all picked up their ears, when, from the head of the table, he said:

"Boys, I ain't no right to ask you to take such risks for me. I'll not hold it against any of you, if you pull out to-night."

No one spoke for a moment.

"I'm curious to know jist what you'd do, if we did?" asked Tex suddenly.

They got some idea of just how bullheaded Hale was in his answer, "I'd do my best to put the herd on myself!"

"You won't even be able to be there," Tex pointed out.

"I'll be there, in any case!" Hale said firmly. "I'm drivin' up in the sled."

"Waal, so will I be there," Tex said quietly.

And they all said, "Same, here!" to a man.

"But so will Kinney's men," reminded Dell's partner, "an' it's time you wise us up to your plans."

"Plans!" Hale's scornful rejection of that dumfounded them all. "I ain't got any plans. What I got is a law-proof right to Thunder Brakes! We'll all go up at sunrise, cut the wire, an' drive the herd on! If Kinney opposes us, we'll fight! He's been dog in the manger long enough. He knows he can't make his claim stick. He's jist tryin' to hold possession long enough to ruin me. But if he drives me out of the country he won't need Thunder Brakes!"

They could hardly believe him as stupidly, criminally, stubborn as that—that he'd persist in his rash course to the point of sacrificing his men.

"You're the general," Tex said harshly, and over his features fell the dark shadows of mystery and gloom. "But suppose you git the herd on—how do you aim to hold it?"

"Possession's nine points of the law," Hale said doggedly. "Jist the same, I'll take precautions to insure the tenth point. I'll have men up there to stand day an' night herd. They can live in that ol' line cabin I built up back of there, years ago, when it was open range. I'll take up beddin' an' grub on the sled."

In a silent body, the Curly Q crew went to the bunk house.

"Feel fit?" Dutch asked Calliope, emptying the shells on his bunk to clean his old six-gun.

"Fit for treason, strategem, an' spoils!" was the stout-hearted reply, as old Cal put in some repairs on his own.

"Strategem!" Dell broke out bitterly. "It ain't much Hale's usin'. Possession may be nine points of the law, but what'll Kinney's men be doin' while we git possession!"

Again the wonder of that stilled them all.

Presently, Tex shivered into his mackinaw, and picked up his hat.

"Where you goin', pard?" Dell's heart sickened

at sight of the gray misery in the face Tex turned to him.

"Back out there," he cussed. "Left two heifers bogged down in a drift. An' I think it's jist as well to take a pasear out there to-night an' see how things look. Pard, the time's come to take things in our own hands. But don't worry. Shoulder to shoulder, we'll win out—we always did!"

Dell's heart bled for him. He'd have gone for Tex, only that he must do night work himself, if he was to be at Thunder Brakes at sunrise.

He was hard at it out in the feed yard a half hour later, when Hector pussy-footed up to him in the dark.

"Dell," he whispered mysteriously, "want to see something funny?"

Glad to have gained his confidence at last, Dell said, "Yeah."

"Then tag along, Dell. Mind—not a sound!"

And Dell did so, careful to step in the boy's tracks, to obey every caution, till, out by the horse corral, he was signaled to stop.

"Look, Dell!" chuckled the boy in a whisper. "D'ja ever see the beat of that!"

Dell looked, and was stabbed to the heart!

For there against the rails, in the glow of the moon on the snow, was the girl he loved, held tight in the arms of his partner.

Tex, bending his dark face to June, hesitated, as in some premonition of them——

"Remember the Alamo!" fiendishly shouted the youngster, thinking it was courage Tex lacked.

Startled, Tex and the girl sprang apart. For an endless and ghastly moment, the partners stared at each other. Neither spoke. But all the while Dell's brain was screaming words—words—— " 'Sure, pard, this ain't the rock on which we'll split? Dell, *there ain't many things in this world that's sure, but you can be dead sure of that!*' "

Nothing was sure! Dell's world crashed. He had banked his life on Tex's word. A failing bank—a bank that went back on a pledge!

"A *sand* bank!" cried his soul in its black bitterness.

Blindly, Dell swung on his heel and left them there. All night he lay in his bunk, staring at nothing, listening in hope and dread for Tex's step.

The night passed, somehow, but Tex did not come!

CHAPTER X

OVER THE LINE

OVER the frozen range, rode Tex, on that night, when the lowering temperature broke all records of a record-breaking winter. Moonlight struck the crusted snow and sent back a silver glitter. Frost made cold music with its rythmic *creak, creak, creak* beneath his horse's feet. A stiff north wind cut through him like a knife. And all the cold of the eternal space about settled in his bones. But his heart was hot with remorse at what he'd done to Dell.

Dell's face rode with him, haunting him with its accusation and reproach. Tex reversed the scene—put himself in his partner's place, and saw just how it looked to Dell. Once he stopped, resolved to go back, and shed the burden of things he'd always meant to tell—things that pained and shamed, but didn't pain and shame as much as having Dell think—well, what he must be thinking.

But, no, he had important business now. He didn't dare go back. He'd have to let that drift to-night. He'd see Dell soon, and then he'd tell him—what he hadn't told him at the depot, and now wished to goodness he had.

He hadn't meant to tell June. But when she brought the sandwiches he'd asked her to make up for him out to the corral, and had been so worried about his going out to-night, why, he'd lost his head and told her.

He'd stand by June, like he told her he would. Stand between her and Jeff Hale's selfishness. He'd take her away—yes, and Heck, too, the little rascal—and let Hale know just how *that* felt, when it happened to him!

Thinking thus, Tex reached the dark, timbered ridges above Thunder Brakes. All about him, trees popped and cracked in the intense cold, as if a guerilla band was fighting there. The sounds struck more terror to his soul than if it were an army of guerillas, all sharpshooting for him. For the bravest man has a secret fear, and Tex feared cold. He could have faced a firing squad without turning a hair, but it took all his courage to face this devastating night.

Descending the eastern slope over the trail the cattle had made, he caught above the wind's wild moan, the cold moaning of the herd. Presently he sighted the dark mass of cattle in the shelter of the cliff, milling in a huddled throng, seeking the warmth of each other's bodies, all covered in the same blanket of white, backs humped to the cold, eyes and nostrils rimmed with frost, giving them the appearance of strange spectral monsters, shrouded in the ghost raiment of snow.

Tex saw beyond them, the horse herd, stamping miserably, and his heart went out to it. Like most cowboys, he loved horses and hated cows. Like all true horse lovers, he held horses little less than human. And these strays of the range had served him faithfully, and at great sacrifice to themselves.

Tex stopped at neither herd, but, circling both, went on. His horse was floundering now in the unbroken snow—for the trail stopped with the horses, and his objective was the west fence of Thunder Brakes. The fence that was the dead line and within which, lay life for the Curly Q herd, and trouble for its men. The fence Rush Kinney guarded zealously by day, but which had no guard to-night!

No rancher would ask a cowboy to ride fence a night like this. No cowboy would do it, if he did. Moreover, no cowman in his senses would endeavor to move a herd on such a night. Certainly not a herd in the shape the Curly Q's was in. According to all logic, the fence was safe till daylight, making it now, as a swift reconnoiter showed, safe for Tex!

"Possession's nine points of the law!" muttered the Texan, halting at the dead line. "An' at midnight the lease goes into effect!"

He hadn't realized how cold he was from riding, till he dismounted and stood knee-deep in brittle snow before the fence. His feet felt wooden. His hands, fumbling a pair of nippers out of his pocket, were wooden hands. Nor could he use the nippers with his glove on, nor get it off, until he gripped his right hand with his knees and jerked. In doing this, he dropped the nippers and, cursing his clumsiness, must fish for them in the snow. Then he had to beat his arms about his body to make his blood race, and restore feeling to his hand.

Now, with only the cold stars to watch and blink at man's audacity, he reached for the taut and gleaming thread of frosted steel that was the top wire of the boundary fence. Seizing it in the nipper's jaws, he brought all his weight down in the pressure.

Z-zip! loud on the frozen silence, the upper strand whipped back.

Clip! Zip! the second writhed away.

Z-zing! and the bottom wire lashed back in snaky coils.

And to Thunder Brakes, the bars were down!

Putting on the stiff and snowy glove, Tex rode back to the horses, and started them toward the fence. Much handling, much starving, made them as easy to work with now as sheep. There and back he drove them, and there and back again, till he had extended the wide trail they had broken from the Curly Q Ranch, well past the gap in the fence.

Now the horses had served their purpose, and he was through with them. For them there was no reward, but freedom to suffer, freeze and starve. But

Tex knew they wouldn't freeze or starve. For God loved horses, too. And He had put the stuff in them that could stand hardships. They could be the help to man they were, and not a drag on man, like the helpless, bawling cows back there. Just the same they deserved better, and Tex told them so, hazing them toward open range.

"If I had a million," he promised, "you wouldn't want. I'd lead you to green pastures down in——" His voice broke queerly. "Beat it, fuzz-tails!"

And he scared them toward the hills.

Now he was ready to complete his job. *His* job—to put the cattle on Thunder Brakes! Why? And again why? A tremendous job, even for a crew—to move this herd at night. A superhuman job for him, with the cold the awful, killing thing it was.

"How cold *is* it?" Back at the Curly Q, Dutch stuck his head above the blankets to inquire of Cal, who had grumbled out of them to replenish the bunk-house fire.

"Ungodly cold!" was the fervent reply.

"I know that!" pleaded Dutch. "But I want it official! Look at the thermometer, can't you? A body likes to know how much he suffers!"

With bad grace, Calliope picked up the lantern and poked his nose outside. "Thirty minus—an' still droppin'!" He groaned on his way back to his bunk. "Heaven pity the poor sailor out on a night like this!"

Yet Tex was out in it! Tex, who couldn't get acclimated—who couldn't stand cold—who was worn out from having stood so much!

"I'll put 'em on myself!" he vowed, riding back to the herd. "Fat chance *we'd* have in broad day, with odds three to one, an' us with our hands full of cows, and the Box Bar fannin' these open flats with their guns! Won't let Dell an' Dutch, an' Cal suicide here, doin' it for Hale!"

No, he wouldn't let anybody else suffer for Jeff Hale!

"I got the right!" his lips twisted in bitter sarcasm as he quoted Hale's supper speech. "'I'll jist go up at sunrise, cut the wire, an' drive 'em on.' Merely that an' nothin' more! Easy as pie, an' simple as Simon! Like heck!"

Hale knew better than that! He knew the risk—had spoken of it, given them an "out," which he blamed well knew they weren't the kind to take. So he'd do it alone! And while the ranch crew slept, gaining strength to do, the group of them, what Tex intended doing alone, he went work, taking grim pleasure in the act.

Just *how* he did it, will never be told. No one was there to see, and Tex could never tell. For his mind was on the dead line, too! And though they saw with breaking hearts the results of that night's work on him, he could never separate the grains of truth from the chaff of disordered imagery that filled his brain.

The cattle didn't want to move. *That,* Tex remembered well. Also, that he had to quirt them into action, and keep at it till his arms seemed breaking at the sockets. Let him get some moving, and others would stop, or stumble off the trail and mire in a drift and sulk. And each time he had to swing a rope, frozen, stiff as cable and heavy as lead, over frosted horns, and swing his horse and yank the stubborn brute back in the trail.

He had to do this over and over, till his brain reeled under it. Until, for weeks, he wrestled and hauled and lifted all the cows born to aggravate a puncher since time began—and could not rest. Did this off his horse and on, freezing, in such agony as few men know, telling them, through tears that froze and seared his eyes like fire, how Heaven helped those who helped themselves. And pleading, praying, with them through stiff lips, for Heaven's sake to help themselves and him!

He cursed them for dumb, stubborn brutes, as mulish as Jeff Hale. And he cursed himself for having the same dumb, mule streak in him. Else why was he doing this? "What," he cried to the pitiless night and stubborn herd, "has Hale ever done for me?" He cried this, awfully, afterward; and Hale cried, too, as Tex answered, then, as now, awfully: "Nothing! An' that's—why!"

He cursed the snow that threw up a thousand hands

to grab his legs and pitch him into it. Yes, first and last, he cursed the snow.

Down on the Neuces, he remembered, lashing the toiling leaders through the gap, they didn't have snow—not to speak of. He'd heard how beautiful it was—how a little of it covered a multitude of rubbish, and made the world all white and new. He'd hankered to see a real fall.

But when he *felt* it, he'd have run like a panther, only he didn't have the cash and couldn't leave Dell. Then when he got the money, and Dell in the notion, he saw June and couldn't go! He wasn't sorry, savvy! He'd freeze his hands and feet plumb off for June! But that didn't cut any ice with snow, nor make it warmer.

"S-snow, s-snow, beautiful s-snow!" he whimperingly quoted, staggering through it to goad some stragglers toward the fence. *"Beautiful*—Sam Houston! Poets may have a license, but they got no ***right*** to lie like that!"

Then, getting down in it to bodily lift an old cow that wasn't worth a half-second of such toil, he feared he'd been too hard on the poets. He was afraid of getting as narrow as a boot lace, like Jeff Hale. Poets didn't *all* like snow. They had tastes like regular humans. And he chanted with ghastly gayety:

"Some like it hot, some like it cold, some like it in the——" Yeah, there was one in his old school reader, who felt just like he did about it. And he racked his brain for that sentiment:

> "'Tis a fearful thing in winter,
> To be shattered by the blast,
> An' to feel the ragin'——"

"Don't I know it!" he moaned.

But he decided, as he got into the saddle again with difficulty, that it wouldn't be so bad, if he didn't make such a fuss over it. Folks *did* live through it. This State was as populous as Texas—more so, he believed.

"It's hot"—gamely he endeavored to fool himself—"hot as Hades! This ol' steer I'm lambastin' is plumb laid out with heat. My clothes is stickin' to my back. The sand's burnin' the shoes plumb off my feet. I'm on the trail to Rio! See the heat waves dance! Git that whiff of chaparral a-scorchin' in the sun——Oh, shucks!"

An hour later the last cow was harried through the gap, and the Curly Q herd was on Thunder Brakes!

"How did you ever git 'em over?" Tex was often asked.

"*Carried* 'em!" he'd say grimly, and there was more truth than poetry in that.

The cows stood on the wind-swept barrens, with bunch grass high, thick, and black, above the thin covering of snow. No stronger stock feed is known to man. Could the herd but stay here, it was safe. But what of Tex?

The numbness of hands and feet had spread deadingly through his body. His brain, having finished the job he had set it to do, was benumbed. He recalled vaguely that Hale had spoken of an old line cabin somewhere up here where he might take refuge, but it didn't occur to him to look for it. It was only when his horse stopped and wouldn't move, that he saw a cabin.

"More sense than me," he praised his mount for stopping before the very door, "but that—ain't sayin' —much!"

Almost falling from the saddle, he staggered to the door, and reeled within.

Pale, gray light streamed through the window, through which the room was dimly seen. Looked "lived-in," the thought struck him, as if the Box Bar men had been using it of late. But he had eyes only for the stove and the wood stacked behind it, and groped about, cutting shavings and laying a fire. He was an eternity getting it started. Then he had just enough sense and self-restraint to keep from it. For his extremities were badly frosted, if not frozen. He found a basin and, taking it outside, filled it with snow.

It took an age of agony and time to take off his felt boots and heavy German socks, that he might rub his feet with snow. He could have screamed with pain, as his blood began to circulate and agonizing life came back to them. But when this pain had abated in a measure and his feet were dressed again, his head fell forward on his breast, and he slept.

He woke with a nervous jump, his hand on his gun, and the sickening realization in his soul that his fingers were too stiff for straight shooting. If the Box Bar men beat the Curly Q here, he must be in shape to meet them and hold the herd!

"Gotta git my trigger finger limbered up!" he muttered, bending to put more wood on the fire; but in the act he started nervously again.

For the sound that had disturbed his slumber was repeated—a plaintive little nicker.

"A heck of a waddy, I am!" he cried, conscience-stricken. For the first time in his life, he'd sought his own comfort before looking out for his horse.

Bent on making instant amends he tried to rise, but fell back groaning, his muscles on a strike. He tried again, and made it painfully.

Through the gloom he could see the feeding cattle scattered out over the slopes below. And hoped they'd get a "skinful" before the fun began. Begging his horse's pardon, with an humble and contrite heart, he took the bag of oats he'd brought behind his saddle and gave it the feed of its life. Reminded of the lunch June had put up for him, he decided to "put on the nose bag," himself.

"Yeah," he said, turning back to the cabin, "I'll

eat, drink, an' be merry by the fire—ready for Bat! I've got possession! See if he's man enough to put me off!"

He reached for the cabin latch, lifted it, opened the door, and walked into *a gun!*

A girl held the gun, and she looked quite capable of using it, though the need was not apparent. For Tex looked as though he was about to drop dead with surprise. A girl in this out-of-the-way spot, at this unearthly hour, would have been surprising under any circumstances. But he hadn't been ten feet from the cabin door, nor out of it ten minutes. She couldn't possibly have come in. But she had to come in to get in—reasoned his whirling brain—unless he dreamed her now. And, barring the gun, she was the kind he'd always dreamed! Still, she didn't look as though she'd come, but always been!

By that Tex meant that this girl—in fawn-hued velvet blouse, and short, fringed, deerskin skirt, with great, black eyes, and lustrous, black, bobbed hair—was too lightly clad to have come in out of the night, and he could see no sign of heavier apparel in the room.

"If you move," promised the girl behind the gun, "I'll shoot!"

CHAPTER XI

BETWEEN DAWN AND SUNRISE

IT was a full moment before Tex found voice.

"If you do," he pleaded, with a ghost of his old smile, "please aim a mite higher, so I'll pass out quick! I've sure suffered all I crave to for one night. An' shoot if you must, this ol' gray head, but for the peace of the soul you're doomin' to eternal perdition, *don't*—till you tell me how you got here!"

The black eyes, aimed on him as unswervingly as the six-gun, flashed.

"It's more to the point," the girl said crisply, "that *you* give an account of yourself—and *pronto!*"

Admiring her technique with the gun, as one good craftsman admires another, he complied:

"I'm Tex Rankin——" All his weight seemed to have gone to his head for his bow was twice as low as he intended, and failed of being utter prostration only by the lucky fact that he still held the door.

"Cow waddy extraordinary for the Curly Q," he continued, "but a long way from home. I'm considered a saint by my friends, an' a holy terror by my enemies. But, between us, miss, I strike a fair medium. An' I swear it's the first time a lady ever found it necessary to take a gun to me!"

The black eyes were decidedly less hostile, though this happy change was not affected by the deep reproach Tex managed to inject into that last.

"When a man walks into a strange house in the dead of night, scaring two women, living there alone, half out of their wits"—it was a mystery how a face made for friendliness could be so stern—"he can expect to have a gun taken to him!"

The mere thought of an offense so heinous, horrified Tex.

"If a man done that," he said warmly, "shootin's too good for him."

"You did it!" She was merciless. "We heard you come in, and there was no way to get out of our room, except through this one—past you—so we stayed in there, still as mice, afraid to make a sound. My gun was out here, and when you went out just now, I made a dive for it!"

There was something pathetic in the big puncher's distress.

"Miss," he said with slow earnestness, "I don't savvy this yet! But if I done that, I rise right here to apologize fast an' fervent. I'm sorry as sin! If I felt any smaller, I'd plumb disappear. If it would help any, I'd bump my head on the floor, ache an' all —an' it sure aches aplenty! All I can say is, I'm innocent of any such intention. I had night work to do, an' my boss told me he had a cabin up here—— This *is* Thunder Brakes, ain't it?" he asked as if he might even be mistaken in that.

"It is!" the girl firmly assured him, though her eyes twinkled. "The cabin Hale spoke of is off north."

"Then I'm in the right church, but the wrong pew!"

"You're in wrong all around!" she flatly contradicted. "For Hale's men have been warned against trespassing on my homestead!"

She saw the tremor that shot through him.

"Your homestead!" he gasped. "Why, I—I thought it belonged to Kinney. Calliope said it belonged to some of that devil's tribe!"

She must have seen that he was not responsible for the uncomplimentary way he clothed his speech, for without the slightest resentment she laid the gun down on the table and said quietly, "I'm Janice Kinney."

And while Tex recovered from the shock, she surveyed him with a woman's sweeping glance.

Lately, she had heard a lot of the two new cowboys who were pulling the Curly Q through by sheer force of brain and brawn. And especially of this one—"Hale's hired gunman," the Box Bar crew called him. She'd had daily reports of his progress toward her homestead with Hale's herd. To her father's men he was an unknown quantity, and they feared him. In this same uncertainty, in the strange magnetism he had for all, lay his fascination for her.

"Mr. Rankin," she said seriously, "the best service you can render Jeff Hale, is to warn him to keep his cattle off Thunder Brakes!"

Dully, he told her it was too late—the herd was on.

She stared at him, incredulous. And he pulled the door wide, showing her the miserable cattle, feeding out there in the dark dawn.

"I brung 'em over last night," he said unsteadily, holding to the door for dear life now, for the room was going round. "I brung 'em over so's to have 'em here the minute the lease took effect. I done it on my own authority—Hale don't know it yet. I—I'm sorry, if you don't like it, miss. I—I'd rather be friends with you, than be—in Texas! But they're here, an' they've got to stay, an' there ain't any help for it!"

He stepped aside, as she closed the door and faced him.

"I'm sorry, too," she was as frank as he, "but you'll have to move them!"

"Where?" Tex asked bluntly, braced against the table now. "Back to the Curly Q? They couldn't make it! What good would it do if they could? Miss Kinney, Hale ain't no feed, an' hundreds of cows back there need it! These are the flower of the flock. Judge by these what the rest are like! I—I ain't the heart to move 'em! The heart was plumb—froze out of me—last night——"

Suddenly he was aware that she was looking at him

strangely—as June had looked at him last night, when she begged him not to go; as his mother had looked at him when he was a kid and had the measles and they thought he'd die.

"You're sick!" she said anxiously.

Fiercely he denied the charge, though her kind glance and tone all but unnerved him.

"You're chilling!"

"I'm a Texan," was his simple explanation of that.

She came straight to him, the last vestige of hostility gone, and laid her hand on the terrible throb above his eyes.

"You were out all night—working that herd over?"

He nodded.

She scolded him for risking such exposure, and the pity behind her words, brought tears to his eyes. Despising his weakness, afraid of breaking down and making a complete fool of himself, he took up his hat.

"If you'll forgive me for breakin' into your home," he entreated, "I'll slide out."

But she put her hand on his arm restrainingly, "Wait!" And, turning about, she called sharply, "Mary!"

Slowly, an inner door that Tex hadn't noticed last night—behind which, to his everlasting shame, two women had barricaded themselves, in terror of him—opened, and the frightened face of an old squaw peered in.

"Come out, Mary," Janice could afford to smile

now at her companion's fear. "It's just a Curly Q puncher—drifted here by mistake. Come, and help me get breakfast."

As the Indian woman sidled out, keeping a furtive eye on their strange guest, Janice affirmed, rather than invited, "You'll stay to breakfast."

Sam Houston! How Tex wanted to. But a certain stubborn honesty would not permit it. He was at war with the Kinneys. He couldn't break bread with——

"Thanks!" his sincerity robbed his speech of stiffness. "Reckon I've imposed on you enough. June put me up some lunch, so I'll jist slope along up to the line cabin an'——" He halted lamely, seeing laughter in her eyes.

"I'm not trying to bribe you," Janice smiled. "You're sick, and you need a hot meal. In simple hospitality, I'm going to see you get it. I may be arming the enemy, but if I can risk that, surely you can!"

Tex had neither the will nor strength to protest longer. And he sank down by the fire, watching the women prepare the meal. He wondered how Rush Kinney could be the skunk he'd imagined and have a daughter like that. Wondered how he could ever have mistaken this place for a line cabin. For now, with yellow lamplight aiding the dark dawn, he saw that it was heaven—Tex's idea of heaven, *home!*

For Janice Kinney had the "home" touch—that

subtle art that can glorify the humblest cabin. The cozy cheer, together with the fragrance of coffee and frying ham, stole upon his senses, and he slept. He dreamed she came to him again, and laid her soft, cool palm upon his head, and said to Mary, "He's burning up with fever, now."

When she called him to the table, it still seemed a little dream of heaven that he was here, breakfasting with Janice Kinney, and the old squaw, Mary, waiting on them both.

The strong coffee put new heart in him, cleared his brain, and dulled the ache; recalled him to the danger that grew with every moment. He remembered now to listen keenly for every sound without. Even to seem not to do so, but to be giving all his attention to his pretty hostess, making conversation of the one interest they had yet in common—the Hale-and-Kinney feud.

She told him of its beginnings, three years ago this very night. For it was at the Thunder River stockmen's first annual dance, that Jeff Hale had insulted her, and they were celebrating the third to-night. Insulted *her!* Yes, hadn't he heard? Jeff Hale had called her names, just because she danced. As if *dancing* was a crime! And when her father demanded an apology, he'd refused to give it. Which they considered the worst insult of all.

Tex had listened, speechless with shame and anger that any man should dare insult her. He suddenly heard himself proclaiming loudly that she should have that apology if he had to drag it to her by the scruff of the neck, then froze into silence at the realization that his brain was running wild.

She told him of the strife, since. And in her eyes Rush Kinney was a martyr, blameless, long-suffering, but goaded at last into taking his own part.

"We're so tired of being blamed for everything that happens to the Curly Q." She seemed desperately anxious to make this strange, still fellow understand. "Jeff Hale blamed us when his cattle stampeded. They ran over a bluff, and a lot were killed. He blamed us when his hay burned last fall. I suppose," she sighed, with a sad, little smile, "that he blames this hard winter on us, too!"

As Tex still said nothing, her eyes were cloudy with resentment.

"You think I'm being one-sided!" she accused him. "You think I'm not fair!"

Tex denied that. But he did think Rush Kinney had kept the facts from her well.

"Jeff Hale started this feud!" she insisted, pouring more coffee for him, and putting more of the biscuits and fried ham on his plate. "He fenced in Cayuse Springs, and cut us off the best part of the range. We *had* to homestead Thunder Brakes."

"*You* homesteaded it!" Tex said abruptly, and after so long a silence, that Janice laughed merrily.

"You've got *that* straight anyhow!" It was wonderful to have her laughing like that, right across the little table from him. "I took it up for dad, because he had already used his homestead right, and needed Thunder Brakes for a range reserve. Unluckily, we didn't inform ourselves about school land, so Hale was able to lease it. But we have a lawyer fighting it now. And in the meanwhile, we're not going to let Hale run us out! Our men are coming up this morning to see that he doesn't——"

"Won't you be here?" Tex was praying she wouldn't. How could he fight her father, with Janice looking on!

"No, I promised dad to come over home right after breakfast," she told him. And he knew Rush Kinney meant to hide from her what happened on Thunder Brakes this morn.

"You see," she must have sensed his thoughts, "I have to stay here nights to establish residence, but I spend most of my time over at home. I won't be here to-night, though, for I'm going to the dance. It's at the schoolhouse—just a step from the Box Bar. So I'll spend the rest of the night there."

As they rose from the table, all friendly confidences ceased. This man was no longer Janice Kinney's guest, but her foe. But when, thanking her again and again, Tex moved to the door, his weaving gait denoted such utter exhaustion, that she relented enough to insist that he go right back to the Curly Q and get to bed.

"Let our men drive the herd off," she suggested, unconscious of the grim humor in that. "You're in no shape to do it!"

Sweet as was her concern for him, Tex's pride was stung that she should think him weak. He wanted to tell her there was "a lot of kick left in the ol' hoss yet," but that didn't sound like anything you should tell a lady, and while he was trying to phrase it more elegantly, she bade him good-by.

She seemed so distant then, and Tex couldn't bear it. He must bring her back to him.

"Not good-by," he said hoarsely as his tired eyes appealed her, "jist—so long! I'll see you at the dance."

Her breath caught sharply. A Curly Q puncher at a dance! What would Jeff Hale do! What would the Box Bar men—— *No!* He mustn't come! But he *was* coming. More, he was pleading——

"Save the supper dance for me!"

The sheer audacity of that stunned her. The supper waltz that time-honored custom holds sacred to one's escort!

"Will you?" he stepped nearer.

"Certainly not!" her head lifted haughtily. But his eyes held such a look of pain, strain, patient endurance—she hardly knew what—that she softened her refusal. "That's Bat's dance."

The idea of Bat Rouge having any privilege with this girl, angered Tex, out of all reason.

"How come it's Bat's?" he demanded harshly.

Face to face with the question, Janice wondered, too.

"Habit, I guess," she mused, more to herself than him. "Bat takes me, so naturally, he reserves that dance."

Tex's face darkened. "If Bat's a habit with you," he said tensely, "he's a bad one—break it!"

Angry now, herself, she retorted, "That sounds like a jealous dig!"

Pain swept the gray pallor of his face.

"If you ever see one grain of jealousy in my make-up," he cried hoarsely, "take that gun to me—an' use it! My opinion of Bat won't bear mentionin', but I come by it honest, an' it ain't—that!"

Through Janice's chagrin that she had inferred him to be jealous of her, flamed a great desire to know why he couldn't be.

"If you loved a girl," her sweet face was very earnest, "wouldn't you be jealous of her?"

Again, from his eyes, his soul in a dark mood shone through. "An' make the one I love suffer!" was his fierce repudiation. "That ain't *my* idea of love!"

A silence fell between them. Old Mary, "riddin" the table, shook her head profoundly over this prolonged leave-taking.

"Will you dance the supper waltz with me?" he pleaded again.

His very persistence won her.

"Bat's jealous, if you're not!" she warned him. "If I do, it means a fight. And I won't be fought over any——"

"Janice"—how naturally her name fell to his lips—"*will* you?"

He swayed as he asked it, and, thinking of the trouble impending, of his condition, of the little chance there was of him being there to claim it—yet thrilling, too, with intuitive knowledge of what he'd go through to claim it—she said fatefully, "*If* you come!"

A strange radiance lighted the Texan's face, and he promised softly, "I'll come!"

In sudden alarm for him, she told him she hadn't meant it to sound like that—like a dare. She meant he mustn't come! He needed rest, and——

"I'll come!" he promised again, and left.

He'd go! Tex vowed that as he reeled out to his horse. He'd dance the supper waltz with Janice, if there were a thousand herds to battle for to-day, and all the Bats this side of the hot place to fight there to-night! But, Sam Houston, how his head ached! Like a husky blacksmith was shoeing the mule in him—splitting his head wide open, knocking everything he ever knew plumb out of his mind. He mustn't let that be knocked out—about the dance. Nor that he had to hold the herd till Dell came! He'd sure be in for it now, if the Box Bar men beat Dell here!

Barely able to stick in the saddle, he rode aimlessly

among the cattle, now feeding in the high rye patches as only a starving herd can feed. Alternately, his eyes strained on the white valley north for sight of the Box Bar men, and the white ridges west for some sign of Dell. Momentarily, the fever grew in his blood, and the white world swam in his vision, fantastically unreal.

Pale streaks of orange stained the eastern sky, and swept the heavens. Sunrise! The hour when the whole Curly Q outfit was to be here to help Tex put the herd on—to settle the right to range Thunder Brakes by force!

Yet, strangely—fatally, for Tex—there was no sign of Jeff Hale and his men!

CHAPTER XII

THE HOLE IN THE WALL

"ALL'S quiet along the Potomac," Tex muttered to his horse. "So we'll find Hale's cabin. Don't want folks to know I walked in on two women. Might bother Janice, an' I don't feel like bein' razzed."

Yes, he'd go up, and start a fire, and let Dell find him there. Dell would be along any time now. To Tex, with trouble breaking, the rest of the Curly Q outfit did not exist. It was Dell, his partner, he wanted at his side.

So he turned his horse up a wild, deep canyon, one of many canyons, and was led by the hand of fate, surely, to that wilderness retreat. Wholly himself, he could never have found it, though he ransacked the canyon from end to end. For he would have been looking for a cabin! But now, with everything strange, his feverish eyes held no fixed imagine of the thing they hunted, and so did not pass over the place, which wasn't a cabin, in the accepted sense of the word, but a hole in the wall!

A door in a cliff, would be a better description. For the builder had utilized a natural rock niche in the canyon wall. Rock formed three walls and floor, necessitating only to roof and front it—which had been done with the heavy slabs of rock right on the spot—to have a warm room some ten feet square. Light came in through a narrow window near the roof, and entrance was gained by an iron-bound door of heavy planks.

Not a soul had been near the place all winter, for the snow, deeper in the canyon, was undisturbed. No one would ever come here, save for a similar purpose. For it was a blind canyon, and devoid of any attraction save this dugout, before which Tex stopped.

As he pushed in the door on rusty hinges, the feeling of complete desertion struck even on his disordered nerves.

"Too lonesome for a pack rat even!" he complained, missing the presence of even one of the faithful little housekeepers of abandoned cabins in the West.

A warped old cookstove, a home-made table, benches, bare bunks, and dry fuel—left by the last inhabitants, as is the immutable law of the range—were the room's sole contents.

Tex built a fire to make it seem he had stayed here, out of the cold. But he didn't hump over it and shiver until chaps and hair were singed. He didn't approach it at all. For Tex—the "fire worshiper," the "vestal virgin" of the Broken Bit, whose heat-resisting qualities were a joke to his friends—was warm! And not one of them seeing him so, but would have thought *this* the tragedy!

For he thought the Chinook had come. He'd never seen one, but he'd heard how quick it made things warm. And he thought it was funny the snow hung on, when it was so warm. Funny how his breath froze, even in here with the fire going. Still, lots of things were funny—like, he grinned foolishly, his letting a girl get the drop on him. Suppose it had been Bat Rouge in there! He'd sure have felt sick *then!*

He wished Dell would come. He couldn't rest till Dell came, and he was dead beat for rest. The comfortless bunk intrigued him. If he could just stretch out a minute, get off his feet. But he didn't dare lie down, for if he did he'd stay down like them ornery cows, and he was responsible for the cows. When Dell came, he'd let him watch the herd, and get some rest.

But he couldn't keep awake in here—it was so hot. He'd get out in the fresh air—go down and look after the cattle. But when he got outside, the air wasn't fresh, but stuffy—hot, too! He'd shed his coat—that would help. Peeling it off, he tossed it back on the dugout floor, made a most ungraceful mount and rode away.

But when he reached a point from which he could see the cattle he didn't feel like going on. No need—everything was quiet. And hot! You'd think the snow would run off in a river, but the sun didn't seem to melt it any. Looking up, he saw there wasn't any sun. The sky had clouded up, and it was "spitting" snow. Maybe there hadn't been any sun. Maybe it wasn't sunrise yet! And that was why Dell didn't come.

Holding to the saddle horn, for things were glimmering again, as through heat waves on a desert, he scanned the ridges west once more for Dell. Sam Houston, how he wanted Dell! But he couldn't see hide nor hair of him.

Then his eyes, coming back, picked up two riders leaving the homestead cabin, and as one of them turned to wave at the lonely figure that was Tex limned up there against the sky, his body stiffened at a thought. That was Janice—Janice and Mary—going home to the Box Bar at Rush Kinney's request. So she wouldn't know what black thing Jeff Hale would have to blame him for to-day! And he mumbled to himself:

"Can look for the Box Bar outfit now!"

This prediction came true with a promptness that surprised him. For as though the girl's going was the signal, four riders swept down from the valley north. And in the lead was the big black that Bat Rouge had ridden into the stable at Blue Buttes. The crisis was here!

In his extremity, Tex's heated brain strove desperately to meet it. One word rang through his brain—strategem! That was what Dell said Hale wasn't using! That's what he had to use—if he kept them from driving the cattle off. He must use strategem, and hold them from the herd, till Dell came!

Boldly, he forced his horse out on a knoll in plain view of the men. And, by the wild yell that went up, by the way they swung their horses and galloped his way, he knew they saw him.

"It's *me* Bat wants—not cows!" he muttered, wheeling his horse about.

Spurring up the dark and winding canyon, he turned at every bend to make sure they followed. And they did! Like a pack of wolves, closing on its prey! The whole mile to the dugout, the Texan lured them.

Here, falling from his horse, he jerked the .30-30 from the saddle scabbard and went in. Closing the heavy door, he leaned against it, panting, trembling, as though he had been running hard. It had come to the fight, and the fight was up to him, but he didn't feel up to it!

"Reckon I can whittle down the odds!" he muttered, his long fingers closing convulsively about the butt of his gun. "Four to one—pie, for a Texan!"

Waiting there, fighting for calm and strength, their voices came to him.

"Tracks show jist one man—*him!*" Bat Rouge's voice was tinged with horrid exultance.

"Go slow, Bat!" cautioned a timid voice. "It's got the smell of a trap to me! First time I ever seen this dump, an' I rode this range for——"

"Slow is right!" an even more timid voice advised. "He's got all the advantage in that fort, an' he's one bad hombre!"

"Got you-all buffaloed, anyhow!" Bat Rouge sneered.

Then Tex heard them draw up before the door, and hold a whispered consultation. At last, Bat bawled a loud halloa.

Pulling himself together by a mighty effort, Tex opened the door.

Bat's face swam before him, bold, insolent, vindictive, but with a queer look that puzzled him. And, puzzled, he saw the same queer look on the set faces of the other men.

He did not realize that he was responsible for that look. That it was occasioned by the awful spectacle he presented, the unearthly aspect of him, with eyes like live brands blazing out of his white and sunken face; blue lips drawn in, wearing a tight and mirthless grin; stripped to the shirt sleeves in the zero weather, and with his gun, swinging low and free, as a gunman wears it when out on deadly business. He did not know he looked at all unusual. He only knew that his brain was on fire—now, when it must be cool!

"Thought you slipped one over on us—puttin' the herd on in the night!" Bat opened up hostilities, but with a certain caution.

Tex made no reply.

"Slip it back, an' make it snappy!" the Box Bar foreman threw caution to the four winds. "The boss said to give you plenty warnin'. So we'll give you two minutes to git started—then we start droppin' beef!"

"That's plenty," said Tex, reaching around the door-sill. "Thanks!"

Bat looked at his men, and his look said, "Bluff!" He looked back at the door, and his jaw dropped, for a rifle had appeared in the Texan's hands!

"Now," Tex suggested softly, *"start!"*

A nameless tremor shot through every heart.

"Shoot!" Tex drawled that mocking invitation. "Don't waste lead on beef! I've won every shootin' match I ever was in. Ain't had a chance to unlimber my gun since I hit this country. An' I'm curious to see if I can git all four of you, before you git me!"

Every man had the sinister conviction that he could.

Bat Rouge, hating Tex, because he felt he'd been hired for the express purpose of exposing him, fearing Tex for the damaging evidence he already had in the train check he had shown him, felt anger rise within him, like a fierce wind rising in the night. Hating him, with black, bitter hatred—because, in watching for Janice to depart, he had seen her wave at him, and knew they had some previous acquaintance, which he jealously pictured according to his nature—Bat wanted to take him, break him with his hands—*murder* him! For he knew his power, and had had time to divine the Texan's state.

"The first time we met," he sparred for the chance to which his blood was leaping, "you said if we clashed, you'd make it worth my while!"

"It will be!" Tex said softly, steadying his body against the door jamb, that he might hide his weakness from his enemies.

"Talk's cheap," Bat sneered coarsely, "but it takes money to buy whisky! A gunman with the drop can afford to talk big. Come out from behind that gun, an' settle it like a man!"

"Like a fool, you mean," corrected Tex in monotonous tone. "I can handle the odds with a gun, but I ain't got conceit enough to tackle four pairs of fists!"

"These men won't interfere!" Eagerly Bat's powerful figure tensed.

"Mebbe not," owned Tex, "but I don't *know* that. I know you're a low-down, double-crossin' lot! I wouldn't trust a man of you, as far as I could throw a cow by the tail!" He had to play his cards mighty careful now! Mustn't let them see his hand and know he had no hand. "Besides"—using strategem again—"I don't want to fight! Might muss myself up with you. Got to look pretty—for the dance!"

Dance! He *was* thick with the girl—*danged* thick—or he'd not risk losing his job with Hale for a dance. He'd made it up with Janice—*his* girl—to go to the dance!

"That's a stall!" Bat's voice shook, and his face was livid.

"Mebbe," Tex spoke slowly now, for he had to search so hard for every word, and then coax his tongue into saying it. "Mebbe, Bat. But you make your men pile their guns on that rock yonder, an' go in the dugout and be locked in till we settle this—an' you'll see!"

Instantly the punchers set up a muttering, and even Bat, wild as he was to get at Tex, drew in his horns.

"It's a trick!" he raged.

Maddeningly Tex admitted, "Sure! A trick to git fair play. Whoever licks, opens that door. You ain't afraid it won't be you?"

"*No,* by gosh!"

Bat was beside himself with fury, and he ordered his men to abide by the Texan's rules.

"He's framin' you, Bat!" one protested wildly. "For all we know, the Curly Q men's hidin'——"

But Bat was master of his crew. "Git goin'!"

he thundered, and the cowed lot, though grumbling still, obeyed.

Sullen, suspicious, they dropped their guns beside the rock Tex had designated, and as Tex, warily watching Bat, stepped aside for them, filed into the dugout.

"Now, Bat," Tex said coolly, "my gun goes in the pile—after yours!"

In his blind frenzy to come to grips with his rival, Bat added his gun to the pile on the rock, and strode back in the trampled snow that would be the battle ring. Then Tex drew the plank door tight, shot the heavy bolt through the staple and not until then did he dump his rifle and six-gun with the rest. With reeling step, and a last despairing look down the dark canyon, he turned to meet the best, most brutal scrapper on Thunder River range!

Where was Dell? This thing between the partners—this bond invisible, but stronger than any steel man ever forged, this bond no man could break—had woman broken it? Had their love for the same woman parted them? Was it this that kept Dell from Tex?

Inside the dugout, the Box Bar men fought madly for the limited window space to view the battle. Not all could see. And the one best situated, broadcast the action to the rest.

"They're squarin' off! Bat ducks that swing! *Wowie!* Bat lands! The Texan's down for the count! No, he's up—he's *down*—Lord, how that man can take it! Bat's got him! Wrong! They're on their feet! They're at it, hot an' heavy—— It's Bat's fight! He's woozy—he—he's *crazy,* boys! Stark, starin'—— For gosh sake, bust down that door!"

CHAPTER XIII

WHY DELL DIDN'T COME

THEY warned Jeff Hale about that slide. Told him the sled could never make it. That it was foolhardy even to attempt it. But in his stubbornness, he could not be dissuaded, and so brought on himself—and not on himself alone, more was the pity—the disaster that kept them from Thunder Brakes that tragic morning.

Only disaster could have kept Dell from Tex. All night, he had listened for his step. And at four o'clock, unable to bear the suspense alone, he had roused the bunk house and told them that his partner had not come home. But the old punchers scoffed at his fears. Leave it to Tex, they laughed, not to monkey with thirty below!

"He didn't want to ride back in the cold," Calliope conjectured, "so he went up to the ol' line cabin to wait for us. He's snugged up there right now, gittin' some sleep—which is more'n I am. Quit fiddlin' around like an ol' woman, Dell, an' git some rest. You're sure a-goin' to need it!"

But Dell's anxiety wouldn't let him rest. He dressed and went out in the dark and bitter cold to do the chores, so nothing could come up to delay them when the time came to start. He tried to believe Tex had taken refuge in the cabin. It was more than likely, for Tex might hate to face him, too, after what had happened at the corral last night, and so have stayed away. But Dell couldn't forget how tired his partner had looked last night. Couldn't rid his mind of the fear that Tex had collapsed—might be lying out there in the snow!

Even more than he had dreaded to see Tex, did Dell shrink from meeting June, and bringing back that agonizing pain. But when he went in to breakfast and saw the reflection of his own anxiety magnified on the girl's pale face, love triumphed over every other feeling, and his heart went out to her. It didn't occur to him that June's anxiety might well be for the outcome of this day—with her home, her father's life, even, in the balance. To him, it was proof of her love for Tex.

He stepped beside her as he left the table.

"June, don't worry," he tried to comfort her, as Cal had tried to comfort him. "He's up at the line cabin now—safe an' sound!"

Her eyes, so strangely blue, looked at him strangely, and her little hand closed tightly about his. Her lips parted, trembled, but words wouldn't come. And then he was gone.

Already, Dell had hooked up the sled, and brought it to the door. Now Calliope and Dutch rode up, their guns strapped outside their coats, their kind, old faces dark with ominous purpose.

Together June and Dell helped Jeff Hale into the sled. Dell mounted then. And June, tucking her father in with nervous haste, whitened as he insisted that she lay his gun across his knees, outside the robes.

"Don't fret, girl," her despair touched Jeff Hale to that speech, brusque, but rarely kind. "Rush Kinney knows I'm in my rights. He'll skedaddle off there quick, once I call his bluff!"

There were more tears than cheer in June's wan smile.

And now they started. But, discovering a stowaway on that sanguinary journey to Thunder Brakes, they had to stop and drag Heck, together with the old blunderbuss he'd smuggled, from underneath the sled, take him back and turn him over, kicking, squalling, mad with mutiny, into the custody of June.

"It's bad luck—goin' back!" superstitiously gloomed Cal. "We'd best all set down, an' make a wish!"

"For Pete's sake let's git started!" Dell was desperate.

The grim cavalcade was off at last—and it was still an hour until sunrise!

Actually on his way, Dell's impatience knew no bounds. His gray eyes strained through the gloom ahead, his body strained in the saddle. With every step the feeling grew that Tex had terrible need of him. He wanted to cut and run—to be there *now* —not snailing along with the sled, as Hale insisted. He found it in his heart to hate Jeff Hale, huddled up there on the sled, holding them all back, like he was so danged important they couldn't get along without him. When all he'd be was a hindrance to them, in their way, as he was now!

They'd told Hale this wasn't any boulevard—this trail made by the stock. But a lot the old Know-it-all cared for what they told him! Well, he was finding it out now! For every few minutes the sled hung up on a tree or rock, and they all had to get down and pull it clear—wasting time, when they ought to be rushing to Tex!

They came to the slide of which they'd warned him, and Dell was sure Hale would see his folly and turn back.

Riding out on it, a little ahead of the sled, he didn't see that Hale had any choice. No sled could stick on the trail, here where it wound around the steep hillside. For the snow had thawed and frozen, till it was a glare of ice, slanting off to the sheer canyon drop below.

Turning back, he was appalled to see the rancher recklessly drive out on it.

"*Stop!*" he shouted. "It's mighty bad here. You can't make it!"

Fatal error—to tell Jeff Hale what he couldn't do!

"Make it easy!" he said curtly, and slapped the reins.

Mentally cursing him for the mule he was, "You'll go over, sure!" Dell warned, spurring back to meet him. "We may be able to pull through the snow above!"

Purple with rage that a mere cowhand should criticize his judgment, Hale yelled savagely, "Git out of the road. I'll make a run for it! We ain't got all day!"

Dell's blood boiled. "You ain't in half the rush, I am!" he retorted, swerving his horse to avoid a collision with the team. "But in this case, it will save time to *take* time!"

It was the voice of prophecy! But deaf to it, as all his life he had been deaf to warnings, the obstinate rancher whipped up the horses and came on. Almost at once the sled slewed and slid toward that deep drop, and Hale, totally unable to control its crazy careening, saw his mistake.

"Two of you ride the runner!" he yelled, exerting all his strength to hold the horses up. "The other grab hold of the rear an' hold on!"

The men were already off their horses. Dell and Calliope jumped on the upper runner, throwing their weight back to balance the sled. Dutch, making a drag of his body, strove heroically to hold it on the trail.

All might have gone well, had not the off horse slipped, and the sudden wrench dragged the other down. Now the frantic struggles of the team for footing, drew the sled steadily nearer the brink, despite the desperate efforts of the men to hold it on. Seeing the inevitable, Dutch and Calliope leaped clear, just as the lower runner shot into mid-air, and the sled, for one split second perilously poised, then toppled into the canyon with Hale and Dell.

For Dell, clinging to one runner, as the other slipped into nothingness, realizing Hale's grave danger, had leaped forward to jerk him from the seat, only to be caught by the rearing frame, and sent hurtling to the same fate.

Shaken with horror, the two old punchers scrambled down. Both men were pinned beneath the sled. And when they lifted it, Dell lay there in the snow, so still, blood welling from a jagged cut in the temple, that they thought him dead. And right there, the loyalty of years notwithstanding, they didn't care how much Hale had fared.

But finding that Dell still breathed, they unearthed their employer from the snow. He, too, was unconscious, and, though no injury was apparent, it was obvious that he was badly hurt.

"An' now," old Calliope lifted his ashen face to Dutch, "where do we go from here?"

"Home," Dutch said wearily. "We gotta git 'em home."

"What about Tex, though? What about the herd?"

"The herd's safe, as long as it stays on the range,

an' it'll have to stay there now, for there ain't nobody to put it on. When we don't come, Tex will think Hale changed his mind, an' come along home. This kicks the bottom plumb out of everything! Cal, the ol' Curly Q's gone!"

Miraculously, the team had escaped injury. And at last the old fellows worked the sled across the canyon till they caught the trail. Then they carried Hale out to it, and went back for Dell. When they lifted him, they saw that his arm dangled queerly——

"Broke!" said Cal.

So they ripped siding from the sled, and bound it on to serve as a splint. Then they laid him in the bottom of the sled, beside the man whose stubbornness, rather than their own hands, had laid him there. They covered both with the same robe, tied the three saddle horses behind the sled and started home. So Dell was borne unconscious over the back trail, and it was the only way they could have taken him.

From the window, June saw this solemn return—saw the empty saddles! And, with some wild thought that they had clashed with the Box Bar, and all but the two old men were dead, she flew out to read the story of disaster in their faces, and to frighten them out of their senses by the awful look on hers.

"Thar, thar, honey!" sputtered old Cal, still yards away. "We jist had a spill, an'——"

"Dad!" her eyes dilated on Hale's form in the sled.

"Don't you dare have a conniption," threatened the terrified old puncher, "or I will, too! He's jist banged up a leetle. But Dell's——"

With a moan that echoed in their hearts long after, June fell in a faint beside the sled.

"You blitherin' idjit!" scolded Dutch, leaping down to lift her. "Of all the blunderin', ontactful breaks a man ever——"

"Don't rub it in!" begged Cal piteously. "How, in tunket, was *I* to know!"

But June surprised them by how quickly she came out of it, taking charge with a swift efficiency that kept them on the jump. Dell was made comfortable on the couch in the living room, and Hale put to bed. Dutch raced off to Blue Buttes for the doctor. And every one had his hand and heart so full there was little time to think of Tex.

But about noon Hale rallied enough to realize the situation. Right or not, he couldn't buck the Box Bar now. He'd lost the fight. He was ruined. He even took a perverse pride in the thoroughness of his ruin. And, in this spirit, he sent for Calliope.

"Go up to Thunder Brakes," he ordered from his sick bed, "an' tell Tex what has happened here. Tell him I said to come home!"

Calliope left on his errand.

It had begun to snow—a fine, steady drizzle that threatened to keep up. June, keeping frantic watch for Calliope and the doctor, saw that hourly the clouds thickened, darkened, with the weight to be disgorged.

For grim old Nature was putting the last of her ammunition into this final charge to be fired, with such terrible effect, in her inexorable, horrible war with man!

CHAPTER XIV

TO THE DANCE

CALLIOPE was the first to return, and with astonishing news. June was lighting the lamps, when he came storming in, but she dropped everything to fly after him into her father's room, and hear his unbelievable story.

"The herd's on Thunder Brakes!" Cal was still so astounded himself, that he must sputter and choke to get it out. "He put it on hisself—in the night! He's fought the Box Bar hisself—Bat Rouge, an' gosh only knows how many more! But they ain't there' an' the herd is, an' so is Tex! So he musta licked 'em, though I couldn't git any details. Couldn't git a thing out of him, that had a lick of sense to it! He's mad as a Hopi medicine man—rantin' about ham an' heaven, an' Fourth o' July! An' a-runnin' around in his shirt sleeves——"

"What!" That fact struck Hale, as it did June and the boy, strangest of all.

"In his shirt sleeves!" vowed Cal, crossing his old heart, his eyes agog. "As sure as I'm a livin' man, an' hope to be till I see this thing through! I'd say he was drunk as a b'iled owl, if he was within twenty miles of hooch! Barrin' that, boss—he's crazy! He—he looks like something the cat drug in! Wouldn't even let me git down off my hoss. Something about him plumb scared me stiff! Told me to git to 'ell back here, and send up some grub!"

Hale's reactions to this story were characteristic. He was neither grateful to Tex, as June and Calliope were, nor did he share their alarm for him. He was mad clear through, at what he considered an assumption of authority.

"He's took a mighty high hand for a cow-punch!" he tossed in his rage. "He's took a heck of a lot on himself! Got my herd up there where Kinney can kill the last cow, before I can git it off! For I haven't men either to git it off, or hold it there! I don't *want* it there!" he cried stubbornly, as sure of that as his obstinate nature would permit. "I won't *have* it there! You go back up an' tell that shorthorn to come down here, an' git his time!"

"I'll be danged if I will!" rebelled Cal, outraged. And, leaving Hale to get over the shock of his first mutiny, he stalked out with as much dignity as a pair of very tired and bowed old legs can muster.

"Lemme go!" pleaded Hector, wild to be at the scene of the fight—with Tex, who was more than ever his hero now. *"Please,* dad, lemme go!"

"Go!" Hale gritted. "Tell him to come back an' git his pay. I'll take no back talk from him *this* time!"

Before the words were fairly out of his mouth, Heck tore from the house, saddled his pony, and galloped off into the storm.

Twilight merged into dark, and anxiety settled as palpably as the dark over the Curly Q.

The doctor—a big, jovial bear of a man—arrived soon after Heck left. He found Hale suffering only from a terrific shaking up and shock. But this on top of his old injury was bad enough. Dell was cut and bruised about the head where the iron work of the sled had struck him, and his right arm had two bad breaks.

The pain of setting his arm brought him to. Then he was like a wild man when he found that night had come, and Tex was not there. Calliope's story put him in a frenzy. *Tex,* in his shirt sleeves! The long strain, hard work and cold had turned his brain. They didn't tell him that Tex was fired—only that Hale had sent Heck for him. He could hardly wait for them to return.

Dell tried to get up, but weakness made him dizzy, and he lay back, hating himself for his helplessness. Tex had double crossed him. That hurt. But he didn't blame Tex any more. Tex loved June so much he'd forgotten the pledge, forgotten his partner. He might have done the same thing himself, with Tex's excuse. For June loved Tex. Dell had seen that in the beginning—at the depot that night. He'd shut his eyes to it—fooled himself. But his eyes were open now—to see his loss!

That loss caused him agony, beside which the agony in his bandaged arm was nothing. Constantly, June kept it before him. Being so sweet to him—waiting on him like this. Women were twice as good to a fellow in trouble—the mother in them, Dell guessed. But he wished she wouldn't!

Endlessly, now, his strength growing with anxiety, he paced. Endlessly, he stared out of the window into the blackness, that was as sunshine to the blackness of his soul. Endlessly, he watched the clock. Eight—half past eight—nine—half past—a quarter to ten——

Heavy on his heart struck the hoofbeats of a lone horse!

Then the boy burst in—snow-sheathed, breathless, panting, eyes as big as saucers.

"Oh, golly! Gee! Golly!" he raved in ecstasy and despair. "Why *couldn't* I 'a' seen it! Talk about a lallapalousa! Oh, dang, an' seven hands round, why did *I* have to miss it!"

"Miss what?" Dell cried, hurrying to him.

"Why, the fight!" From Heck's tone, nothing else of import might have happened since the world began. "It sure was a stem-winder! It——"

Sternly, Dell cut in, "Where's Tex?"

"Up there"—Heck's observant eyes had picked up the details Calliope had missed—"all over blood! An' it ain't all offa *him* either! He's got a cut lip, an' —outside of a peach of a shiner—that's *all* he's got! Gee, but I'd like to see Bat! I'll bet he's——"

In his impatience, Dell could have shook him. "Why didn't Tex come back with you?"

"He ain't comin'!" declared the boy with fierce pride. "He ain't the kind you can boss around! He said to tell you, Rush Kinney had come up there, an' he'd fixed it so the cattle wouldn't be bothered. He said don't worry about the herd, he'd look after it! An' he's goin' to the dance——"

"Dance?" Dell thought that blow on his head had made *him* loco!

"Over to the schoolhouse to-night! Goin' over to finish the job!" decided the bloodthirsty youngster. "Goin' over to finish Bat! To clean up on the whole blamed crew. He can do it, too! Dell, listen——"

But Dell was listening to the horrible version of what happened up there, fear created in his mind. Tex—going to a dance! Tex wasn't a dancing man! He'd dragged Tex to every dance they'd attended since they were partners. Nothing could make him go—sick, worn out, as he was—unless he felt he had to go.

That was it! He'd been dared to go! He had fought Bat Rouge, and from all accounts, had whipped him. Then Bat had dared Tex to meet him at the dance, where the whole Box Bar crew could avenge him. Kinney, knowing Tex was the dangerous one, had granted immunity to the cattle to get him there, where they could gang up on him!

Tex wouldn't hesitate tackling them all. Like he'd tackled that gang of roughs who had waylaid him, Dell, down in Yakima, when they had first met. He'd thought it was all up, when Tex, passing by, saw one man being manhandled by ten, and waded in. Dell saw him now, as he had had an unforgetable impression of him then—lips drawn in, a devil in his eyes, fighting as if he had no sense of fear, of feeling—no sense! Nothing could stop him. Nothing *had* stopped him then—bullets, knives—and he and Tex carried the marks of both. Dell saw Tex now, looking like that, fighting like that, the whole Box Bar crew.

All this flashed through his mind as his eyes sought the clock. It was ten! It would be eleven before he reached the schoolhouse! Tex was there—now!

Snatching up his holster, Dell made the wide-eyed youngster strap it on. Then seizing his coat, he flung it around his shoulders. With his arm in a sling, it wouldn't meet across his breast.

"Button the top one," he hoarsely instructed the boy, "an' let it flap!"

Then he was out in the storm, with Heck hard on his heels.

Calliope was coming up the steps.

"Come, on, Cal!" Dell nailed him. "Saddle my horse!"

The old man peered into Dell's face, saw the look there, looked at his crippled arm, at the gun, with holster hitched to the left——

"What the——"

"Saddle my horse!" cried Dell distractedly, "or I'll jerk his danged hammock off an' do it myself! The Box Bar's got Tex at the schoolhouse dance!"

Old Cal humped himself to obey. Dell plunged off at a gallop. And, bursting with excitement, Heck dashed into the house to tell June.

She was in the living room, staring blankly around for Dell.

"He ain't here!" babbled the boy. "He's gone to the dance!"

"Gone to the dance—a man with a broken arm! That's a story!" Never had June taken that tone to Heck before.

"I ain't storyin'!" he insisted honestly. "He's gone. I told him Tex went over there to clean up on the Box Bar, an' he went like a shot! Gee, I wisht I could go! I can't *ever* have any fun! Just poke around this ol'——" He broke off to stare at his sister.

"Where *you* goin', June?"

She was frantically donning coat and tam.

"Heck," fretfully called Jeff Hale from the bedroom. "What's goin' on out there? Where's June?"

The boy paled, but made no answer. Things he had

often said that were better unsaid, but only in a spirit of fun. He was no tattler.

"June!" called her father imperiously.

Flinging her scarf across her shoulders, and drawing on her gauntlets, June went in.

Suspicion swept him at sight of her.

"Girl," he demanded, "where you goin' at this hour of the night?"

Strangely, in that moment of utter dread, the lifetime habit of obedience broke. Her father's anger meant nothing more to June than any other cause of delay.

"To the dance!" she said fearlessly.

Hale jerked up in bed, his arms raising in a paroxysm of rage, as if he would strike her dead. "Girl, are you crazy!" Wrath all but strangled him. "Git off that coat!"

Undaunted, her gaze flashed full on his.

"Don't you try to stop me, dad! Don't you dare!"

There was that in the blue eyes of the little insurrecto that took Hale's nerve, and he didn't dare. Fear was his one weapon. When there was no fear he was disarmed and helpless. And while he was so, June went.

The sound of her horse racing off came in to Hale. He sat there, shaking, his face hidden in his hands, as if he would shut out something too awful to look upon. Something born in the past was leaping now to terrible maturity. Never would she give him unquestioning obedience again. June was lost to him. And he knew in his soul that it was retribution! The blow he had once struck, exquisitely cruel, ruthlessly brutal, had rebounded on his own heart! In agony, he spent the night. All night, out on Thunder Brakes, the white snow was sifting, steadily sifting, covering—whatever was out there to cover!

CHAPTER XV

THE WALLFLOWER

ON with the dance! Do your worst, Old Winter! Spread death and desolation over the frozen range! Bury it deeper, deeper, deeper, in the white ashes of the hopes you blast and ruin! Who cares? Just for to-night, trouble is left out in the cold. Young hearts beat hot. Old hearts are young—just for to-night! For the flower and chivalry of Thunder River range is tripping the light fantastic at the stockmen's annual dance at the little schoolhouse on Badger Creek. Hearts beat the higher, feet trip the lighter, for what has been and what will be. On with the dance!

"Git your part-ners for the nex' quadrille!" calls the caller in a foghorn voice.

How the pretty girls dimple and blush, and gaze everywhere but at the cowboys swooping for them in one grand rush—looking to the boys like posies in a garden waiting to be picked. And each picks his favorite, while plump, fond mammas, ranged along the wall, beam with pride. Papa, grandpa, even the baby, watch and beam. For the gang's all here!

And grandpa's feet hitch as "Yakima" Joe, "The

Fiddlin' Fool," gets in swing, bringing down the bow in "Buffalo Gals" in a way to bust the stoutest string. On with the dance!

"One more couple needed here!"

Another couple coming, hand in hand.

"Everybody ready? Yeah—all set!"

"Everybody dance as pretty as you can,
Turn your taws an' left ala-man!
First couple balance, an' first couple swing,
Promenade the inside ring!"

Mad, merry bedlam of fiddle and laughter and promenading feet. The devil's pastime? Heaven save the mark! A little interlude of wholesome fun in a hellish six months. Sanity, for some! They dance, the winter-weary, work-weary, heart-weary! They dance, the ruined—and so forget!

"Down the center, an' cast off six,
Lady to the right, an' gent to the left,
Swing at the head, an' swing at the foot,
An' the sides stay put."

Grizzled old stockmen, watching the heated swirl, can't *quite* forget!

"Make it, if the Chinook comes soon," over the hubbub, one allows. "Tight squeeze, though! How 'bout you, Sam?"

Sam sighs and shakes his head, as white as winter, and twice as white for the winter outside, "Too late for me—if it come to-night!"

"Tough luck!" they all tell Sam.

"Uh-huh," he owns, though their sympathy makes it a lot less tough. "But it could be worse. I ain't the cows to lose Jeff Hale has, an' I hear he's——"

> "Down the center an' cast off four,
> Lady to the right, an' gent to the left,
> Swing when you come together ag'in,
> An' everybody swing!"

And everybody in the whole three sets dizzily swings. *"Buffalo gals, ain't you comin' out to-night?"* screamingly inquires the violin. They play as they work, with the last ounce of vim. And the fiddler fiddles away like mad. Fragrance of coffee, drifts out—incense on the altars of appetite. Noses of hungry punchers twitch. Clatter of dishes and feminine tongues, as the womenfolks—too old to dance, and wise enough to know it—fix supper in the cloakroom. For the supper waltz comes right after this quadrille!

Cowboys, "smoking out" this dance, gravitate to the smell.

"What's wrong with Bat?" asks one gay-bandannaed young slim-Jim. "He ain't come. First dance I ever knew Bat to miss! An' Janice here, too!"

They'd all been wondering about that. What, indeed, was wrong with Bat? Not only with him, but the whole Box Bar crew? They usually led the herd at every dance, but not a mother's son of them was here to-night! Nobody from the ranch at all, but Janice and her ma! Something wrong, sure!

"Must be trouble at Thunder Brakes!" predicts a purple-chapped buckaroo. "Heard Hale was puttin' stock on to-day!"

"Then *that's* where Bat is"—affirms another—"seein' he don't!"

"Hear about the wild Texan Hale's got gunnin' for Bat?"

"Circle eight, when yuh all git straight!"

Wistful-eyed waddy, with his eyes on Janice over by the wall, speculates wistfully, "Some chance for the rest of us mebbe—with Bat not here!"

"No chance!" his bunkie, as wistfully, sighs, "Janice ain't dancin' a-tall!"

"A wallflower—*her?*" The first waddy scorns the thought.

"Waal, 'tain't *my* fault!" on the defensive, his friend declares. And they all laugh feelingly, for it wasn't theirs!

It was one of the world's great mysteries why Janice wasn't dancing, *wouldn't* dance! Sitting there so still, the lily of the garden, where she had been the rose—for even the pink of her frock lent no warm glow to cheeks robbed by some nameless emotion of their natural pink—Janice was wondering why she came, and why she stayed, with her mother begging her to go.

For her there was no music, sparkle or life. She might never have danced. For her there was nothing but the door. And she watched that intently, fixedly, as a crystal gazer watches the ball for some mystic reflection of fate.

Ma Kinney, watching that door as eagerly, broke under the strain.

"We'd better go, Janice!" Rising, she reached for her wraps, hanging on the wall above her. "Somethings' happened—I *feel* it. Your father knows how nervous I am. He wouldn't stay away like this. He never stayed away before——"

"Wait, mother," Janice's voice was as weary as her cheeks were pale. "Wait!"

Ma Kinney looked at her with worried mother's eyes. What was she waiting for? For whom was she watching like that—Bat Rouge? Ma Kinney didn't like that. She didn't like Bat! Maybe it was for her father, Janice was watching so white and still. No—for him she'd go home and wait. Rush wouldn't come here.

"I declare to goodness," she fretted above the

beat of fiddle and feet, "I don't know what's got into you, Janice! You've done nothing but stargaze the livelong day. And you *would* bring me here, when I was half wild about Rush——"

"Wait!" colorlessly, the girl implored. "Just wait till——"

Then her heart stopped beating, for the door was swinging in! It wasn't Fate—or was it?—but three Box Bar punchers framed there.

"Here's the boys, mother," she cried eagerly. "They've found dad!"

The quadrille had broken up on a burst of laughter, and the crowd on the floor was so dense that it seemed an age to Ma Kinney before the snow-covered boys could elbow through. And then they brought no news of Rush Kinney, Bat Rouge, or any of the missing men.

"We've fine-combed the country from here to Thunder Brakes," Lou, a strapping big fellow, confessed with reluctance. "Can't pick up a sign of them. Hale's herd's down there, but there ain't a livin' soul with it!"

"Don't worry, mother!" begged Janice, not taking her fascinated gaze from the door. "Dad's probably home."

"He ain't!" Lou denied soberly. "We stopped at the ranch when we come by. They ain't showed up there! We found—— Nobody ain't heard a thing at the ranch!"

"Lou," Ma Kinney's quick ear had caught that break, "you're keepin' something from me. Don't, Lou! Anything's better than this suspense! You found——"

"Jist their horses!" blurted the puncher. "We found 'em standin' saddled, at the gate!" And he felt like a criminal, as the woman whitened, and sank back on the bench, moaning:

"That terrible gunman has killed them all!"

"Nonsense!" cried Janice. "He's not terrible, mother! He's——"

"Supper waltz!" announced the caller. "Every hombre dance with his own!"

Young hearts beat furiously now. Blushes deepened. Dimples danced. The supper waltz—which time-honored custom holds sacred to one's escort!

Oh, how intently the great, black eyes watch the door now! He'd come, he said. She had promised!

"'Tis the last rose of summer, left blooming alone,'" sang the violin hauntingly sad, sweetly subdued, after the abandoned hilarity of the quadrille.

Not to miss one throbbing, pulsating moment of it, the floor fills. Slowly, happily, dreamingly, the waltzers circle past. Every hombre with his own.

"'When true hearts lie withered,'" sang the violin to Janice, "'and fond ones have flown, oh, would inhabit——'"

"Dance it with me, Janice—Bat ain't here!" gulps a blushing cowboy, with his heart in his eyes.

"Thanks, Dave, but I promised it!"

Then Bat *was* coming! But the dance went on and on. Half over, and Bat hadn't come——

"Let's finish it, Janice," the diffident one returned.

But she didn't hear him. And if she had accepted, he would not have heard!

For the music had stopped on an agonized squeak, and everybody stopped! Everybody looked toward the door, as though the fate of every one was reflected there—and it were a horrible fate!

Horrible, the fateful figure, steadying itself against Old Winter, who was having the first real look in. Hatless it was, and coatless. With shirt all but torn away, and horribly smeared. With hollow eyes burning the dead face up. Fireful eyes, that scorched all they touched. That touched all, in a slow, laborious search of the throng.

By the big, black six-gun, worn low, with holster point strapped down, they knew him. And Lou's hoarse mutter: "Jeff Hale's gunman!" spread and spread.

The mutter broke in a gasp of horror as the eyes found that for which they searched, and the terrible figure reeled across the room, to halt, swaying before Janice Kinney, and thickly murmur, as if with a great effort, "My—dance——"

But not to claim it! Pure grit could carry him so far, but no farther. His knees sagged, and he caught desperately at the wall for support. His burning eyes were bent on the white-faced girl shrinking from him —shrinking, with crazed wonder at whose dear blood he might be stained with, and horrifying her still more was his thick-tongued murmur, "Bat—bad habit —Janice—broke it——" As, slowly, his hand slid down the wall, and he crumpled senseless at her feet!

Instantly, the place was in an uproar. The nerve of him! To come here in that shape! To approach Janice Kinney for a dance! Angrily the mob closed around him. Gunman, or not, they'd show him——

"Throw out the drunk!"

Hands that wouldn't have dared touch him, had he been able to lift a hand, were laid violently on him——

"Drunk?" screamed Janice Kinney, her scorn staying those violent hands. "Can't you see—— Oh, you fools—he's dying!"

Not dying, if Ma Kinney could help it. Not with that secret locked in his breast. He knew where Rush was. Oh, too well, she feared he knew! And she was down beside him, ministering to him, as if she would hold him to life by force.

But just at first the awful significance of the hideous blotches on his white face and shirt, was too much for even her great fortitude, and she covered her face with her hands and swayed to and fro, moaning.

"He's been in a fight—terrible! He won, or he wouldn't be here! He's killed them all! Oh, Rush, Rush——"

"There's jist one way he could do that!" Lou said shakily. He drew the Texan's gun from its holster and broke it. He looked at the full chambers, through the smoke-free muzzle, held against the lantern light.

"Cleaned recent!" he grated.

What was there in *that* to make a hombre's blood run cold?

"What's up, Lou?" somebody asked for the crowd.

"That's what *we* want to know!" grimly retorted the Box Bar man. "Rush Kinney, Bat Rouge, an' some other men went up to Thunder Brakes this mornin' to guard the fence against the Curly Q herd. They didn't come back—but their hosses did! We've rode since three o'clock lookin' for 'em, but the ground might have opened up an' swallowed all four, for all we found. This fresh snow's wiped out every track. But this hombre was up there, an' he knows——"

"Won every—shootin' match—ever was in——" deliriously Tex muttered. "Don't waste—bullets—on beef—where I come from——"

Spellbound by that ghastly revelation of an uncensored mind, they stared down at him.

None saw Dell enter—to start and freeze at sight of that still, prostrate form, the center of that tense ring.

"Who done it?" they heard him utter in a cracked voice.

They saw him now, with awe—a figure scarcely less

appalling than Tex had made, his arm in a sling, his head and face a crisscross of plasters, his gray eyes blazing with wrath such as few men know, and which was as strange to Dell. And they drew back as he slowly crossed the room, stood over the still form of Tex, and, looking not at him, but hard at them, again in that wrath demanded: "Who done it?"

The deadly ring of his voice, the way his left hand hovered at his gun, made them fear they had been mistaken—that *this* was Jeff Hale's gunman!

"Nobody done it," wearily, Ma Kinney answered him. "It's pneumonia! I know—for I nursed Rush through it twice."

All at once, Dell was as weak as he had every right to be. He dropped down beside Tex, the last trace of resentment, of hurt, even, vanishing as he looked into his face.

Tex could break all the pledges man ever made. It didn't matter. Tex was his partner! But there was something stamped on Tex's face now that seemed to put the seal to their partnership. A great bitterness welled up in Dell, that Tex wouldn't know it didn't matter. A great desire to call Tex back and make him understand.

"Tex!" he cried, wringing tears from every eye there. "Tex—ol' pal——"

Tex's eyelids fluttered. Dell never knew the effort Tex unconsciously made to lift the weight of them. But Dell heard his broken whisper, "Pard—knowed—

you'd come——" And he rose blindly, as Tex fell back in a coma that was close twin to death.

It was so close that June, breaking through that circle—the third tragic figure to enter that door to-night, her snowy little tam pulled every which way, her blue eyes, big and black with dread—could not tell them apart. And, grief-stricken, she pushed Ma Kinney aside, taking Tex's bloody head in her arms, sobbing over it as if her heart would break. Sobbing in a way that broke Dell's heart.

Dimly he was aware of a girl in pink, gently lifting June, and drawing her gently away from the curious throng; and of that girl's strange-toned query: "You love him?"

And June's anguished, "Oh, Janice, Janice, *so* much! I've wanted him all my life! Prayed he'd come! But not—for this——"

Moving away, Dell ran blindly into a barricade of Box Bar punchers.

"Now," ordered Lou, throwing a gun on him, "we'll hear from you! Talk, an' talk fast! Where's our men?"

Dell stared at him blankly. "How should I know?"

"You danged well know!" Lou cried coldly. "They went up to fight you yahoos! You an' your pard have been in a scrap—you shore show it with your face worked over, an' that busted arm! You're here to tell the tale, an' our men ain't. So git goin'! If you tell us nothin', we'll treat you rough!"

A lot Dell cared. But he didn't have the heart for more strife.

"I ain't been within five miles of Thunder Brakes to-day," he said dully. "I been in an accident."

"Uh-huh," drawled Lou, with fine sarcasm. "I suppose you run into a buzz saw—jist by accident!"

Too weary to argue, Dell told him of the accident with the sled. Told him the movements of the Curly Crew that day. That they knew there had been a fight of some sort at Thunder Brakes, but——

"You know as much about that, as we do!" he concluded. "I've told you the truth. Take it, or——" Then Dell's apathy fell from him like a cloak.

Lou was stepping aside, to make way for men, who were carrying Tex out!

"Where you takin' him?" Dell blocked their way.

"To the Box Bar!" one said grimly.

A red haze swam before Dell's eyes. "You're not! Not by a——"

"Oh," broke in Lou meaningly, "we'll take good care of him—precious *good* care—till he tells us what he done with Kinney!"

They would have had to fight it out with Dell, then and there, crippled as he was, but for Janice.

"We're not heathens," she told Dell, with a quiet force that beat through his fury. "The Box Bar is nearest, and he's too sick to be moved far. If he's your partner—come, too."

So Dell, who had headed one grim cavalcade on that day's dark dawn, now in its night, rode with another, more sad, more grim. He rode beside the sled that bore his partner and the girl he loved, who loved his partner, over the hill to the Box Bar Ranch!

CHAPTER XVI

DELIRIUM

DELL never forgot that night! He lived a lifetime in it—waiting there, suffering and on sufferance, in the Box Bar parlor. His ears were straining for every sound from the bedroom beyond. His eyes searching every face that came out of it, for the hope he hungered for, or the news he feared. He caught a glimpse, now and then, as the door opened, of June's face, set in a grief that shut the door of heaven on him.

Faces came and went, but with never a sign for him. The Kinney women had forgotten Dell in their anxiety, so much greater than his. But the Box Bar men remembered him too well, and their faces were hostile. Dell felt that, were it not for the women, they would, indeed, have treated him rough. He didn't care. They could put him on the rack! Wasn't he there already? What wouldn't he give to change places with Tex? To be dying, maybe, but with June to grieve! No, he didn't care what they did to him, as long as they took good care of Tex. And they sure were taking care of him.

"Like he was the Lord Heir Apparent!" grumbled

Lou, carrying a cot through the parlor, into the bedroom, for Ma Kinney's use. "Stretched out in the best bed. Togged out in the boss' nightshirt! Like he was the son of the house, instead of the skunk what brought trouble on it!"

"I'd sure admire to have the handlin' of him!" vowed the waddy upholding the other end of the cot. "I'd nurse him into talkin' sense—an' pronto! If Scotty don't bring news of the boys, when he comes back with the doctor——"

"Fat chance!" Lou scoffed. "You know blamed well they wouldn't 'a' gone to Blue Buttes!"

"I know!" was the grim retort. "But when he gits back, the women will know! Scotty'll inquire at the livery barn, an' a grasshopper couldn't come in town, but Curious would know it!"

Dell heard, but he didn't blame them. He'd felt the same toward a Box Bar man suspected of having done away with his pals. Nobody knew what had happened to Kinney and his men—unless it *was* Tex. And Tex couldn't tell!

Suspense had the whole place upset. Every one was running about, stopping at every sound to look and listen. At every moment the strain grew.

The all-but-intolerable throb in Dell's arm forced him to lie down on the couch at last. Despite the pain and strain, he must have dropped off, for he found himself suddenly sitting bolt upright, listening to voices outside.

"Any news?" That was Lou.

"Not a whisper!" That must be the cowboy whom they had sent for the doctor. "They ain't been in town. Nobody's seen 'em on the road! Looks bad, boys! The sheriff reckoned he'd better come out an' join in the search. He'll be here——"

Janice was bringing the doctor into the parlor. And he had symptoms of apoplexy at seeing his Curly Q patient here.

"What you tryin' to do—finish the job?" he growled, taking off his gloves and rubbing his hands at the fire. "Don't you know there's easier ways to kill yourself? You go to bed and stay there a year. Vamose!"

But the cowboy could only say dazedly, "My pard's in there!"

"The one you were having hysterics about, when I left you at the Curly Q?" asked the physician, more gently.

Dell's white misery was answer enough.

"Say, that's bad!" the doctor's sympathetic pat wasn't professional. "We'll take a look at him, and ease your mind."

He went into the bedroom with Janice, and again Dell was left alone to wait. Sometimes, he heard Tex's voice raving and the doctor's low rumble. But mostly he heard nothing at all. It seemed to him he couldn't wait. A dozen times he walked to the door and put his hand on the knob, and a dozen times went back to the couch. But, after an age, the doctor appeared in the door.

"Cold packs to reduce the fever," he instructed Ma Kinney and Janice, who were following him out. "Nothing much I can do. The main thing is to keep his heart up, and I've left digitalis for——"

"Is it pneumonia, doc?" Dell couldn't wait any more for that.

"Yes—and a bad case," the doctor said gravely. "But see here, young man, you get to bed, or you'll be down yourself!"

Then he, too, forgot Dell, as the women beseiged him. For Scotty had told him just what the situation was here.

"How long before he'll be rational?" was Janice's white-lipped query.

"That's hard to say." The doctor tugged at his beard. "He's not apt to be rational until he passes the crisis—in from five to eleven days."

Ma Kinney's cry was heart-rending. "If he shouldn't get well," desperation was in her whisper, "will he be able to talk before he—goes?"

"Not likely," the doctor was forced to tell her. "He'd sink gradually. But"—quickly administering a hypodermic of hope, and thereby cheating himself out of another patient—"I'd listen mighty hard to him now. He's talking drivel, of course. But he might drop something that would give you a clew."

He slipped into his coat. "I'll be back to-morrow."

Adding, by way of a tonic, "I bet I find Rush here, big as life and twice as natural. So long, folks!"

For moments the sound of his horse loping off, was the only noise heard in that room.

Five to eleven days to wait thus! Five to eleven days to listen for a loved step, loved voice. Five to eleven days to wonder if they were dead or alive. If alive, to live with the fear that eleven—or five days even—would be too late! And the only hope, in the meanwhile, would be the meaningless mutter of a delirious man!

"Would you like to go in now?" Remembering him in their sharpest grief, Janice asked Dell the question.

So he went at last into the Box Bar guest room—never, *never,* intended for such a guest! But Dell wasn't thinking of the singular fact that Tex was their guest. He wasn't thinking of a thing, but that this couldn't be Tex—this wasted shell of a man, fever-flushed, and with eyes that held his gaze.

He couldn't think of a thing about Tex's eyes, but the ridiculous thing Little Red Riding Hood asked the wolf that had swallowed her grandmother: "What makes your eyes so big and bright?"

And the wolf's ridiculous answer, "The better to see you with, my dear."

What made Tex's eyes so big and bright? The

better to see—what they couldn't see? What were they seeing—Tex's eyes?

Sitting in the chair that Janice had drawn up for him, beside, Tex, opposite June, Dell wondered what made Tex breathe like that—so thin and fast—as if it were hard work just to breathe? What made him keep on talking that way—as if his tongue hung on a pivot and wagged at both ends. Now—when he had a chance—why couldn't he rest!

Dell had to listen to him, though he didn't want to. He hadn't the reason for listening that the Kinneys had. And it was killing him by inches to listen to his pard.

Poets had lied to him, Tex said, for snow was hot—burning hot! They'd buried him in it on Thunder River Range. And he was so tired hunting home, sweet home.

"No place like it, is right!" he complained. "For there ain't no such place to be like!"

Anyhow, *he* couldn't find it, and the Lord knows he'd tried. He'd come to the Curly Q, and it wasn't there. He'd gone to heaven, and he thought heaven was home. Sam Houston, how he wanted it! But there was a black-eyed angel, guarding the gate with a six-gun——

Pitifully rapt, Janice Kinney bent over Tex.

So he'd gone to school. He had to ride seven cows to get there. And they got stuck in the snow. And he kept pulling them out—till he got so tired doing it, that he carried the cows. And the place he came to wasn't anything anyhow but a hole in the wall. There were so many wires to clip, and Bat had stolen his nippers, and gone off on an iron horse, and wouldn't be back till kingdom come. And he was so tired dancing for his supper with June and that sailor, and he couldn't rest till Dell came. And Dell was a long time coming——

All at once, Dell had to get out of that room, or go loco himself.

But back in the parlor, alone, he wished he was back with Tex. He looked out of the window and saw it was dawn. How many years had he lived since last dawn, when he'd been on his way to Thunder Brakes?

What had happened there? Four strong, well men couldn't just disappear. They had to be somewhere! Why weren't they home? Why weren't they found? Far from being the ogre he'd thought him, Rush Kinney was a "home man," every one said. He wouldn't traipse off anywhere without sending word home. Then—why wasn't he home?

To keep himself sane, to lift that awful suspicion from his partner, Dell tried to account for the missing men. He tried to build up out of his knowledge of Tex and what Calliope and the boy had told him, just what had taken place when the Box Bar men went up. He'd heard the punchers, here, talking about Tex's blundering into Janice's cabin up there, and of how he'd left her to go to the old line cabin. But the search party had been to the line cabin, and there wasn't a sign of Tex!

Bat had come, and he'd fought Tex—that much was sure. Kinney had come, and said the cattle wouldn't be bothered—— No! That was what he'd made out of it himself. Dell racked his brain for the boy's actual words: "Tex said to tell you"—Heck's shrill treble seemed right in the room—"that Rush Kinney had come up there, an' he'd fixed it so the cattle wouldn't be bothered!" *Tex* had fixed it!

A deathly weakness came upon Dell. A thousand instances of Tex's unbelievable recklessness flashed into his mind. He'd fight to the death against any odds—one man, or four, it wouldn't make any difference to Tex. Suddenly, Dell was no longer alone. For something black and monstrous drifted in from out there to bear him grisly company.

After all, what did he know of Tex? He knew there were secret chambers in Tex's heart, locked to him. There were depths to his nature that Dell had never penetrated—but he knew Tex wouldn't do *that!* But what of Tex before he came North? What brought him North? "A family matter," Tex had told him at the depot, that "hurts heaps"! That was the only time Tex had mentioned his family. He always talked like he was a stray. Where was his family? Oughtn't it be notified——

Janice was coming into the room, but Dell didn't

turn. She couldn't have much use for him. But he worshiped her for what she was doing for Tex and June. Instead of showing the least animosity, she'd been just like a sister to June!

She stopped beside him at the window, searching the gray horizon, and Dell's heart swelled to bursting, as he realized for what she searched.

"Can't I help?" he begged huskily. "Can't I do something?"

She answered him gently, "You'd help me?"

"I'd die for you!" he cried tensely. "For what you're doin' for him!"

His extravagant speech brought a wan smile to her lips, though she knew it was the literal truth. Still in her little pink party frock, made for laughter and music and love, she studied the Curly Q cowboy with serious eyes.

"Then tell me," she faltered, "hasn't he said something to you—haven't you at some time planned something together that would give us a clew?"

"Nothing," he denied honestly. "Goodness knows, I'd tell you if we had! I've been turnin' my brain inside out, but there ain't a thing. You see, we didn't plan a thing, but to put the herd on—an' fight if we had to. We didn't know Tex meant to do it himself. Nor that he had done it, till Calliope came back, like I told you. An' we didn't hear anything more till Hector came back in the evenin' an' said

Tex was goin' up to the dance——" Suddenly, Dell stepped toward her, his face transfigured.

"You've thought of something?" Janice cried, with the lilt of hope. "What is it? Quick?"

"Tex didn't have a thing to do with it!" Dell couldn't tell her fast enough. "Tex wouldn't have gone to the dance, if he didn't think the Box Bar crew would be there! Why would he? He didn't give two whoops about dancin', an' dog tired an' half sick to boot——"

"He went," Janice said tragically, for her disappointment was cruel, "because he asked me for a dance, and I promised!"

Dell stared at her incredulously. A man in love might do it. But a man in love with June, wouldn't go for another girl—even a girl like Janice Kinney.

They were silent for a moment. Then Janice gathered strength for the question she'd hunted him up to ask.

"Dell," she bravely lead up to it, "how well do you know Tex?"

And promptly, he said: "Like a book you know by heart!" though he'd just been admitting hidden chapters to himself.

"Is he"—and this took all her courage—"the kind of a man who could do—*that?*"

"Not in his senses!" Dell flashed.

Frightened they stared at each other, like children afraid of the dark. For they shared the terror that

Tex, in his half-crazed condition, had slain them all!

"He didn't!" Dell tried to assure her and himself. "I've looked at his gun an' cartridge belt—they're full! There's nothing to show that he fired a shot. Nothing to show that a shot was fired!"

"Nothing," said the girl wearily, "except that dad hasn't come home!"

Always for Janice that immutable fact remained! She slipped off so quietly that he scarcely knew when she left. He scarcely knew anything any more. He didn't know what to do with himself. His girl, and his partner! What was left? He'd go away. He'd wait and say good-by to Tex. Let him know why he hadn't come to Thunder Brakes. Tell him it was all right—what he'd seen at the corral—all right about June. Then he'd go. Probably he'd be invited to go anyway, for a man with a broken arm wasn't much use on a cow ranch. Besides, the Curly Q wouldn't have much use for men any more, for in a few days there'd be no cows——

A drift of voices from the sick room drew his attention.

Ma Kinney's: "You'd better send for your father, June!"

June's in hot opposition.

Ma Kinney's again: "You'll be sorry, dear, if you don't! An' you're too young to carry a lifelong regret like that!"

Then Tex was dying—certain, sure! That did to Dell what weeks of cruelest toil, the cruelest loss that man can suffer, had not done—beat him down, at last!

June found him on the couch, his heart broken, his face buried on his broken arm. Tenderly she raised his face, wet with the hot tears of his anguish.

"Go home, Dell," she said tenderly, "you can do no good here."

"A lot of good I could do there!" he cried bitterly. "A lot of good I'd be anywhere!"

"You've done a wonderful lot of good for me!" she said tremulously. "When I think of you and Tex, as you were at the depot the night I asked you to come—so strong, so—and as you are now, Dell, I—I ——" She broke down utterly.

"I'd have come jist the same, June."

Her hand touched his, light as a snowflake, but warm, and her touch all but unmanned him again.

"I know," she whispered, "and that's what makes it so hard!"

Because she was sorry for him—knew he loved her. June mustn't be unhappy for him.

"Don't worry about me, June," he entreated, laying his hand on her arm.

"But I do!" she cried passionately. "It's different with Tex. Lots of men would do what he did—it was only natural! But you"—bravely her blue eyes clung to his, glorious with a light that thrilled him through—"you did it, because you—loved me, Dell!"

And he answered with hoarse passion, "Heaven help me—*yes!*"

Somehow, that quieted June.

"Dell," she whispered, "go get dad."

Then the bedroom door closed softly behind her, as she went back to Tex.

June's wish was a law unto Dell, and he put on his coat as best he could to go to the Curly Q.

Coming out in the kitchen, he passed the Box Bar punchers eating an early breakfast, so as to be off at daylight and begin the search.

"That hombre gits my nanny!" Scotty said, as Dell went out.

"Mine, too!" Lou said ominously.

"I mean, how he looks—all broke up, that a way—like he hadn't a friend on earth."

"I'm savin' my sympathy for my own outfit!" was the hot shot Lou took at him.

But Dell wasn't to go to the Curly Q yet. For, leaving the house, he saw Calliope assisting Jeff Hale from the sled. And, hurrying on, intending to make some explanation of the crisis here—the strain this house was under, the shape Tex was in—Dell saw Hale's face, and was stricken dumb.

It was the face of a man who was carried away by some passion within himself. And as, with no sign of recognition, he walked by Dell on Calliope's arm, the cowboy, in rising fear for June, trailed after.

The Box Bar punchers sprang up in outraged

amazement at sight of him, but Hale gave no sign that he even realized he was in the enemy's camp.

"I never thought to darken your door," he told Ma Kinney, who opened it to him.

"You've darkened this house for years, Jeff Hale!" said the woman courageously, twisting her apron in nervous hands. "You've brought this last black shadow on it! Your presence here can do no more!"

Dell doubted that Hale even heard her. "I've come for my daughter," he said coldly. "I'm told she is here. Will you send her to me?"

Then, as if miraculously, Ma Kinney's toil-worn, anxious face softened with womanly compassion for him.

"I'll take you to June."

Dell followed them all down the hall, into the parlor he had just left, but he didn't go into the bedroom. As the rancher made his slow entrance, Dell saw June rise from beside the bed, and over the wasted form of Tex, face him with the same fearless defiance that had marked her first mutiny—the night when her father had ordered her to fire him and Tex.

"Git on your things, June!" The sight of her here seemed to fan Hale's passion beyond all restraint.

"I'm not going, dad!" Oh, the pride Dell had in her then!

"Git—on—your—things!" Many a man would have quailed at that. "I'll have no more of this nonsense! Have you lost your senses? What is this man to you?"

Softly, ringingly, June echoed: "What is this man to me?"

"What is he to you?" lashed out the rancher, with a black fury that made Dell shudder. "Answer me, girl!"

"What is he to me?" reëchoed the strung and quivering girl. Then she begun to laugh. She laughed terribly. After that laugh Dell knew revelation would come of just what Tex was to her. And he was grateful to Calliope for coming out at that instant and closing the door.

Old Cal took one look at Dell's face, one look back at the door, barring the room he'd just quitted, swelled up, and exploded:

"Hell ain't a half mile from here!"

For one hour, Jeff Hale was in that room. In that hour the sheriff arrived with two deputies, to direct a sweeping search for Rush Kinney and his men. Every one was called on to tell all they knew. Calliope was let off easy. But Dell was subjected to a most rigorous questioning, that ended only when Janice unexpectedly came to his aid.

"He doesn't know anything about it," she told the officer. "The doctor verified his story about the accident."

No mention was made of Jeff Hale's presence under that roof. No one entered the bedroom. It was as if the Box Bar was in a conspiracy to keep inviolate Hale's hour there.

But when the horses were assembled in the yard, and the grim riders mounted, equipped for a long search, and steeled to find, what they might find under the sifted snow out there, Dell went back to the parlor.

The bedroom door was ajar. The scene Dell looked upon was one he never forgot, though the glimpse he had of it was brief.

Hale was down on his knees beside the bed, his big frame shaking with sobs, crying that he couldn't stand it, he couldn't stand it——

"Don't dad! Don't!" pleaded June, through her own sobs. "He wouldn't want you to grieve like that!"

And Hale cried in such mortal anguish as Dell had never heard on the lips of man: "That's what I can't stand—that he won't know!"

CHAPTER XVII

HECTOR DISAPPEARS

DELL accompanied Calliope back to the Curly Q. Why? He didn't know. Not to get away from Tex's wild talk—he'd hear that wherever he'd go. Not to get away from June's wild laugh—as long as he lived that would ring in his brain. Just to be doing something, he guessed—anything but wait.

But here, sitting up on the sled beside Cal, he was waiting again. There wasn't a thing to do now, but wait. Everything had been done!

Silently, they bobbed over the white road that dipped down the white valley between the hills. The sky had emptied its snow. And a strange, sullen blue dropped out of the sky and veiled the hills.

"Turnin' warm," Calliope pointed his whip at the blue.

But Dell didn't look. He didn't care.

On the last rise, he gazed down on the Curly Q. From the hill opposite, he and Tex had pulled up to look at it—could it be just three weeks ago? Then it had seemed cold and lifeless to Dell. Now it was a hundred times more so. For the snow, thick-strewn over all, was the white ashes of his hopes, too.

As they drove down by the feed yards, Dell saw the Curly Q herd—that part of it which had been his charge. He saw it with more horror than when first he'd seen it, and with more cause for horror.

"The hay's gone?" he asked Cal, well knowing it was.

Cal looked grave. "Every smidgen! Give them their last feed this mornin', Dell!"

As they climbed to the barn, clear on the silence that fell between them, came the ring of an ax. Old Dutch, down there in the bottom, slashing. Not released, as he'd hoped on the first of March, but shackled the tighter. Why was he doing it? What did he hope to do? Cut brush for his herd, and Dell's too? What were men made of, Dell wondered again, that they worked like that? They didn't know when they were licked! And he knew now, men were made of metal as fine and hard as that ax! Metal that rang as true as Old Dutch's ax.

But Dutch had better rest. These cows were doomed. So were those on Thunder Brakes. The Box Bar men would be certain to drive them off and adrift to-day. Hale was ruined, no two ways about that. Dell was sorry for him, sorry for June, and a little bit sorry for himself, too. It was making it hard for him to leave. He hated to leave a sinking ship. Still—with this smashed arm and all—wasn't he just another dead weight to drag it down?

Where would he go? Back to the old Broken Bit?

No—he'd always be reminded of Tex there. He'd strike out on his own—Texas, maybe. That would be funny—if he went to Texas, and Tex stayed here! Yeah, funny as Tex laying up there——

"Oh, gosh a'mighty!" groaned old Cal, pointing at the little chapped figure flying to meet them. "What we goin' to tell Heck about Tex? *Who's* goin' to tell him? Not *me,* by a jugful!"

Neither did Dell have the courage.

"Why tear his li'le heart out?" tempted Cal cravenly. "It'll be soon enough when we have to. What he don't know, won't hurt him, Dell!"

Before Dell could figure out what was best, the boy jumped up on the runner.

"Where's Tex?" he cried eagerly. "Was he at the dance? Did he clean up on the Box Bar?"

Helplessly Dell looked at Calliope, but the old man was singularly busy with the reins for one driving a docile team up a steep hill.

"The Box Bar wasn't there," Dell said haltingly, keeping his eyes from Heck's. "The crew's turned up missin'—nobody knows where. Nobody can find them," he continued elaborating on this to keep the boy's mind from Tex, "an' the sheriff's got a search party out now."

"Sure they can't find 'em!" Excitedly Heck climbed into the sled, and sat down on the dashboard, looking straight up at Dell. "Tex cleaned up on that

outfit! He'd bury 'em deep! Dell, who can't they find?"

"Rush Kinney, Bat Rouge, an' some other men—Mojave, they called one——" and, seeing the boy's eyes fill, Dell remembered Mojave was Heck's old pal, and was sorry he'd blurted it out that way.

"I wisht"—Heck was looking away, but Dell saw his little chin quiver—"I wisht I'd 'a' told Tex to lay off Mojave."

To keep him diverted from Tex, Dell deliberately hurt him. "Mojave sure had it comin' to him!"

Fiercely, the boy denied it. "You don't know a thing about Mojave! He was the best ol' scout! Why, he told Tex to tell me—— Where *is* Tex?" he suddenly switched. "That's *twicet* I've asked you! I wanta know, Dell!"

Desperately, Dell looked again toward Calliope, and again the old man was busy as all get-out with the team.

"Tex was—tired," he fibbed, to spare him. "He went over to the Box Bar to rest up a spell!"

Heck's big eyes looked deep into his, "You're lyin', Dell!"

"I ain't!" There was truth now in Dell's stricken eyes for Heck. "He was so tired—puttin' the herd on an' all. An' there wasn't any place as near as the Box Bar where he could rest. So the Kinney women invited him there. He's there now—with June an' your dad——"

"Did dad an' Kinney make up?" he asked, for that only could account for this startling turn of events.

"You forget—Kinney ain't there." Dell was about at the end of his string.

All of this, Hector thought over seriously, as they pulled up to the barn and unhitched.

"Jist the same," he worried, tagging Dell, "it's funny Tex would go there. There wasn't any sense in it, Dell. No matter *how* tired he was, you could 'a' brung him home in the sled!"

Thinking how soon Tex might be brought home so, almost finished Dell.

"You done noble," Calliope approved him, when the boy was out of earshot. "I couldn't 'a' done better myself! But he's sharp, an' I wouldn't be surprised none, if he smelled a mouse!"

Hector made that clear, by the way he dogged Dell. Over and over, the cowboy must tell him again. Each time, the boy insisted that it was queer Tex would go to the Box Bar—even though the Curly Q hadn't any quarrel with the Box Bar women, as Dell pointed out.

All day he clung to Dell's heels like a shadow. And that day was the longest in all Dell's life. The hungry cows moaned like lost souls in torment. The house was as still as a tomb; and the Curly Q a ghost ranch for sure!

Neither June nor Jeff Hale returned. And Dell, shadowed by Heck, wandered about like a lost soul himself. He did what he could, and was sickened by seeing so much that he couldn't do. And all the time he kept thinking of Tex. He couldn't keep Tex out of his mind.

He lived every moment of their partnership over—tense moments, close moments, moments when Tex was a stranger to him. He even relived the moment he'd seen Tex kiss June. But he savvied that now. Tex was just human—though honest, loyal, and big-souled as a man could be, as he'd showed them all by what he'd done on Thunder Brakes. He wanted to quit thinking of Tex.

Folks said thinking of other people's troubles helped you to keep your mind off your own. He'd think of the Kinneys'—what Janice and her mother were going through, with Rush Kinney gone. They didn't make better folks than the Kinneys. Look how they were nursing Tex! Jeff Hale was to blame for it all. Hale was the meanest man out of jail! He didn't want June to marry, so she'd always be home to keep house for him. He'd sure raise Cain about her marrying Tex——

But why had Hale been so broken up when he saw Tex was sick? What was he afraid Tex wouldn't know? He'd been crazy mad when he found June with him, then why—— What, in that hour, had happened to him? Come to think of it, this wasn't the first time Hale had been broke up by Tex. Tex had broke him up pretty well that night he'd told him some plain truths in the living room and had bullied Hale into letting Tex and Dell stay. He'd had a hunch then, that Tex had an ace up his sleeve which he hadn't played. No use, he couldn't quit thinking of Tex.

"If he'd 'a' been *my* pal," dinned the lad, who couldn't forget Tex either, "I'd 'a' brung him home!"

A reproachful plaint that gave Dell a strange sense of guilt.

One incident—funny at another time, but pitiful now—served to distract Dell's mind for a moment from Tex. Going down to the river, where both old punchers were working like mad, he heard Dutch begging old Cal to sing!

"What?" Cal couldn't believe it.

"I don't give a continental what!" Dutch implored. " 'Polly Doodle,' or any ol' thing!"

Cal had the look of a man who had not lived in vain! Dutch wanted to hear him sing! Then his face fell.

"You waited too long, Dutch," he quavered. "I ain't one of them what sings when they're saddest. Reckon I won't ever sing ag'in!"

Dell went to bed early that night to be rid of Hector's eternal, haunting reproach. And, avoiding him as much as he could next morning, he rode over to the Box Bar, late in the afternoon, to ask about Tex.

He found suspense at the Box Bar doubled both

ways. The search party was still out. Other outfits had joined it now. For Thunder River range was shocked by the strange disappearance of the prominent rancher and his men. There was no change in Tex, Janice told him, and he hadn't said a word that would help.

Dell didn't go in to see Tex. Nor did he see June. But he saw Hale lying on the couch in the parlor, and went in to ask him what they were to do with the starving cattle. Hale was sleeping after his all-night vigil. For moments Dell looked down on him, as at a stranger. His white hair fell back from a face "plumb gentle."

All the mean, stubborn pride was wiped out, every harsh line erased. What magic had wrought this change? And the change worked magic with Dell, for his heart softened toward his employer, and he did not wake him.

The sun was westering over the hills, when he rode back to the Curly Q. He went down by the racks, and the cattle followed him, bawling piteously.

"I've lied to you!" Dell told them bitterly. "I've made you big promises, which I can't live up to. A bullet apiece is the kindest thing I can give you now!"

Calliope came out to the barn, as he rode in.

"How is he?" the old puncher asked fearfully.

"The same," Dell swung off his horse. "I mean, that's what they tell me. But, Cal, he can't be the same. For when a man's as near dead as Tex is——" He whirled at a piercing, wild scream.

There, staring at him in wide-eyed horror, was Heck.

"He's *dead!*" the boy had come in on the last four words. "Tex is dead! He can't come home!"

And he burst into a wild fit of sobbing that terrified them.

Quickly Dell knelt beside him, putting his good arm around him, holding him much as Tex had held him, that first morning, when he'd taken the pitchfork to them.

"He ain't dead, Heck!" he cried remorsefully. "I'm a coward not to have told you, an' spared you this. Tex is sick—mighty sick—but he ain't dead!"

But there was no comforting Hector, and they were helpless before his grief. What is so hopeless as a child's grief? For them, there is no sustaining philosophy, no former experiences from which to draw comfort, nothing but the awful, abysmal blackness of the unknown. And Heck in his grief turned like a wild cat on Dell.

"He was *your* pal, an' you left him there! You knowed they'd kill him! *I* wouldn't 'a' left him! I won't let him die!"

Twisting out of the cowboy's embrace, he leaped on his pony, bare-backed, wheeled it, and raced out of the barn.

"Reckon that's best," Cal said huskily. "He'll feel better, once he sees Tex."

Furiously the boy galloped over the hills to the Box Bar, his tears streaming down his little bandanna, his chapped legs kicking his horse at every jump. Heaven only knew his thoughts! But he thought to purpose!

For, jumping down before the Box Bar, he rushed past the women—who had flown to the door at his hoofbeats, as to every hoofbeat that terrible day—and ran down the hall. Seeing June staring at him from a door at the end of it, he pushed past her, with the same tearful defiance, and burst into the room where Tex lay.

His father sprang up at his entrance, and seized him, lest his presence have a harmful effect on Tex. But Heck fought like a catamount, kicking, biting, screaming that they were to let him go to Tex.

"Let him," June interceded, as the Kinney women came in. "Tex loved him. He has as much right here as we."

Warning him to be quiet, his father released him. But no warning was needed now! Slowly nearing the bed, sight of his idol quieted Heck. How closely death hovered over that bed, even the boy could see.

Tex's eyes were open, but they looked neither on him, nor on any one there. The eyes of every one in that group were bright as they watched the boy—bright with tears that blurred. Through this blur, that made the scene indistinct, they saw Heck lean over the bed, half lay across it, and grasp Tex by the shoulders. Holding him so, before any one could stop him, he piercingly shrilled:

"Tex! *Remember the Alamo!*"

Slowly the dark head rolled to the old battle cry of the Texans. The eyes seemed trying to focus, to reflect something like a conscious gleam. And they heard, or thought they heard, Tex consciously whisper:

"Heck!"

Then the rapturous boy flung his arms about Tex, hid him from their blurred vision. Was it a whisper they heard—broken whispers!

Rushing to the bed, they lifted Heck, dazed beyond all protesting, and stared down at Tex. He had sunk into a lethargy from which nothing could rouse him. While Ma Kinney was still desperately striving, June saw Heck sidling out.

"Brother," she caught him by the hand, and droppe down beside him, "what did he say?"

The boy's face was guarded, for all that the daz wasn't out of it yet. "Nuthin'," he said sullenly "Nuthin'—much!"

"What was it?" June insisted, as the women ran over, frantic with hope. "You've got to tell us, Heck!"

"Honest, sis," protested the badgered boy, tugging away from her, "it wasn't a thing but—words——"

Pressed for them, Hector, like many an adult under fire, couldn't remember.

"It ain't likely he does," Hale said finally. "It's likely jist sick talk—the sort we've been hearin' these last two days."

While they were discussing it, Hector slipped out!

But June wasn't satisfied. She knew the boy far better than his own father did. She was sure he'd heard something.

"He wouldn't have left Tex, if he hadn't," she confided to Janice. "And, whatever it was, he wouldn't tell it—he's far too loyal to Tex."

Together, the girls ran out to hunt him. But he was nowhere in sight, and his horse was gone. So they dispatched a rider posthaste to the Curly Q.

Dusk had fallen when the Box Bar man came tearing up to the house, demanding news of the boy from Cal and Dell.

"He ain't back yet," Dell said, thinking it would be strange if he were. "He's over there somewhere. You couldn't pry him loose from Tex on a bet!"

But when he heard the circumstances under which Heck had left, Dell was wildly alarmed. Tex had told the boy something. Then Heck had turned up missing, too!

"By gee!" Cal vowed crazily, as Dell saddled to ride back with the puncher and join in the search, "I'm goin' to tie a string to the rest of us!"

CHAPTER XVIII

THE CRISIS

THEIR arrival without the boy plunged the Box Bar into the wildest excitement. June was distracted. Where could Heck have possibly gone?

"He'd have to leave tracks," Dell reminded her. "I'll trail him, June."

"How?" sarcastically queried the Box Bar puncher, considering that a slam on himself, for not looking for tracks before he lit out for the Curly Q. "How? With the place tracked up like it is, an' night come on?"

How, indeed!

There was nothing to do, but wait in the most heartbreaking suspense for another dawn.

At six that night, the search party came in, fagged and discouraged.

"We've scoured the range," the sheriff told Mrs. Kinney and Janice, "from Thunder River to Little Klootch Creek. It ain't possible we missed them. They just ain't there!"

He was completely flabbergasted when he heard he had one more to search for.

"Reckon," he pondered, when he'd given it some

thought, "that the Texan told the kid where the men are an' he's gone to fetch them?"

Only that hope made the night endurable. For Tex was sinking.

"It's the crisis," the doctor came out to tell them. "He's fought pneumonia on his feet two days. We can look for the change toward dawn. I'll stay!"

For a while June sat with Dell in the parlor. She sat on the couch beside him, staring with unseeing eyes at the wall, or sobbing her fears.

"He's just a baby!" she'd cry. "He never was away from home overnight in his life! I can't bear to think of him out in the cold——"

"He was bundled up warm, June," Dell would comfort her. "He's as much of a man as any of us. He'd look out for himself. Besides, it ain't so cold now."

Her eyes thanked him.

"Isn't it strange, Dell," she said, growing calm, "how real trouble makes you see clear—like a summer storm washes the haze from the air, and brings the hills near? Here, we've been worrying about the cattle, till this comes along. And now we see it's nothing—nothin, at all, that we've lost them, Dell."

He looked at her quickly. *"Lost* them?" he repudiated. "Not if *they* know it, June! They're tyin' into that hay like they was used to it! I never got so much kick out of anything as the way they——"

"Hay?" The blood drained out of her face. "Dell, are you delirious, too?"

"Good, ol', unadulterated alfalfa!" He saw now that she didn't know. "The Kinneys didn't tell you? Didn't want their right hand to know what their left gave, I reckon. But they couldn't very well hide their hand, for there was a Box Bar puncher on both loads! Maybe you think we didn't do some tall whoopin' when they drove in! An', June, they're lettin' the herd Tex put on, stay at Thunder Brakes!"

June jumped up, and ran to Janice, who was just coming in.

"Oh, Janice," she cried, carried out of her grief by gratitude and affection, "you—you did that! After all——"

"Don't shame me, June," Janice's eyes filled with tears, as she hugged the girl tight, "for *one* neighborly act! We should have shared with you long ago——"

Her head raised proudly as Jeff Hale, who had overheard this through the half-open door, came in. He came in slowly, as though the coals of fire she'd heaped on his head were an actual weight.

"You sent hay to my herd?" he asked her strangely.

"For June's sake," Janice explained, still holding her head high, still holding to June.

"Girl," miserably Jeff Hale appealed to the girl he'd insulted before the whole range, "I ain't any right to ask you to, but I hope you'll listen. What

I say, ain't because of what you did, for I meant to say it before leavin' this roof. I'm a hypocrite! I'm everything you ever thought me—an' worse! I've wore blinders all my life—but that ain't no excuse, for they was of my own makin'. They narrowed my view. Kept me from seein' a thing but myself. They kept out the light of Heaven's sun—happiness, innocent fun. Till I got to thinkin' jist to be happy was wicked! But, thank Heaven, they're off. Janice, I'm seein' clear. An' no matter how much you hate me, girl, you don't hate me as much as I hate myself!"

"I don't hate you, Jeff Hale!" said the girl, deeply moved.

"No," Hale found no consolation in that, "you ain't got the meanness in you to hate. Not even for the vicious way I treated you once. I'll never git over bein' sorry for that. I know it's too late to be sorry—for, if it wasn't for that, these past three years of trouble would never have been. These black shadows wouldn't be over this house to-night! But I—I'm sufferin', too! I'm an ol' man, Janice. Will you—can you, for June's sake, if not mine, overlook an' forgive?"

In her straightforward way, Janice gave him her hand. She had her apology at last, and, though it had come too late, she was too generous, too touched by the rancher's sincerity, to refuse it.

Heavier settled the shadow over that household as

night wore on. No one tried to sleep but the weary searchers. Dell going out with them in the morning to search for the boy, couldn't sleep and didn't try. Tex was nearing the crisis. That overshadowed everything else. *His* heart was not out in the cold with Heck, filled with awful thoughts of what could have snatched him from sight and home—his heart was with Tex. Again, he listened strainedly for every sound from that room. They were all in there—the Kinneys and Hales, keeping their solemn vigil.

For this was more than the prayerful watch over a man's struggle for life. It involved seven lives, and those who loved them. Long ago, Tex had ceased to mutter or move. Would he slip off to the Range Invisible with that secret locked in his breast? Or would he come back?

The doctor held his pulse. Why did he frown as he held it? Was it so faint he must add the sense of hearing to that of touch?

Ages, Dell waited, alone. June had promised to call him at any change, so that, one way or another, he could say good-by to Tex. Every sound seemed to tear the heart out of him, for he thought it was June.

The darkest hour comes before dawn. Night had drifted into that darkest hour. The house was astir now, as the searchers made ready to start at dawn. He ought to go. There ought to be a Curly Q man in the party. It looked like he was a shirk.

"See here, buddy," Lou was beside him, fingers gripping his shoulder hard. "He's your pardner—you stay! I'll take your place in the search!"

Tightly his hand gripped on Lou's, but he couldn't say even as much as thanks.

They left, and the house was so still that Dell heard the clock in the kitchen tick. Not a sound came from in there, where Tex was going through the valley of the shadow of——

"Come, Dell!" June's soft hand slipped within his. He went in with her that way.

Looking at Tex, he knew why she'd called him so gently, taken his hand—pity again! Tex had already said good-by to him! Tex was——

He stumbled forward, to be caught by Jeff Hale and led to a chair.

So he didn't see the doctor lay down the wasted hand, and sigh deeply. But he heard the most blessed words tongue ever uttered:

"He's coming back!"

CHAPTER XIX

A GUARD

UP in the jungle of chasms and crags that lay north of Thunder Brakes, was a wild canyon, one of many similar canyons. And, in it, a cabin—which wasn't a cabin in the accepted sense of the word, but a "hole in the wall." Here, long ago, a fugitive horse thief had fronted and roofed a natural rock niche, making a fortress so perfectly hidden, so well blended into its wild setting, that a man might ride within twenty yards of it, and never detect it.

But no man would be likely to come within even a mile of it, for it was a blind canyon, and devoid of any attraction, but the dugout, whose very existence was unknown. Yet, for years, deserted, "too lonesome for a pack rat even," it was well peopled now!

Men jammed it! Wild-eyed, desperate, half-crazed men. For them, for three long days and longer nights it had been a living tomb. Three days without water. Two without food—the sandwiches they had carried to sustain them in their fight for Thunder Brakes had tided them over the first day. One day without heat—for the fuel, burned with religious economy, had lasted two. And now to the horrors of hunger, thirst and fear, was added the enervating, penetrating chill of their stone cell.

For them, there was no escape. The heavy-iron-bound door—locked on the outside by an iron bolt, driven through an iron hasp—had nobly withstood their frenzied battering. Yet had they broken through it would have done no good!

For, whereas, yesterday, had they been able to break out, they would have been free to leave that chamber of horrors, to-day it would be fatal to go. Whereas, yesterday, they had fought for that bit of window—too small to admit more than one face at a time—to look at the strip of sky, and feast their eyes, at least, on freedom, to prayerfully scan the trackless snow for help—this morning they fought for it to plead with, bribe, threaten, and cajole their guard.

For last night they had been found! But, maddeningly, it had not meant deliverance. Their guard was deaf to reason; indifferent, even gleeful, of their fate! And the day broke over the grotesque spectacle of a boy of eleven in absolute mastery of those stalwart, desperate men!

"Good heavens, this is awful!" Rush Kinney paced his prison like a caged wolf, looking not unlike one, with his sunken, burning eyes and three days' beard. "All that kid's got to do, is lift that bolt out an' we're free! Free to go home—home—home! But he won't! He may pull out any minit an' leave us to die here! Men, when I think of what the folks at home are goin' through—— Mojave, try him again. He's *got* to listen to sense!"

The gnarled, little man with the pallid mustache and cold eye, who had made such a deep impression on Tex, rose from the bench obediently, but without hope.

"It's no use," he told Kinney for the hundredth time. "Heck's got the Hale stubborn streak—only in him it runs to bein' true-blue to his friends. This Texan is his friend, an'——"

"Well, *you* used to be!" desperate, Kinney burst out. "Remind him of it! Put it on thick!"

Bat Rouge, wildest, more nearly crazed than any of them, surily drew back from the window to let Mojave there.

"Heck!"—despite the fact that he was suffering from the boy's obstinacy, a thrill of pride ran through Mojave, as Heck leaped up from his nest of boulders, coolly cocking a six-gun and aiming it steadily—"Heck, be a good scout an' let us out! We'll die in here. We're most froze—most starved, now. A real hombre never goes back on a friend, Heck. Jist lift out the bolt! I'd do as much for you!"

But the boy's heart was set against that appeal. It came nearer breaking him than Kinney's attempts to reason with him, or Bat's awful threats.

"Don't beg me no more, Mojave!" his pitiful quaver gave Mojave a deep sense of shame. "I told you I won't, an' I won't! Tex put you here, an' I'll see you stay! If Tex didn't want you here, he wouldn't have locked you in!"

"He's weakenin'!" Kinney encouraged. "Keep it up!"

"Listen, Heck," Mojave implored. "I wouldn't do *you* this a way! Remember the bows an' arrows I uset to make you. Remember that rawhide hackamore I——"

"I ain't rememberin' a thing!" Heck's little whimper belied that. "I'm sorry, Mojave, but if you will mix with a wild bunch, you gotta take your medicine! It ain't my fault!"

And just as Tex had braced his trembling body against that door jamb to hide his weakness from his enemies, so the boy dropped down behind the boulder to hide his tears.

The scarlet thread of adventure had crept at last into the monotonous pattern of Hector's life. At last he wasn't missing anything. At last, he was having fun! *"Men—hole—in—wall——"* Tex had whispered, and he knew!

For when he had found this place, while hunting bird's eggs last spring, he had named it "Hole-in-the-wall," after a famous outlaw retreat. And he hadn't even told June about it, because he meant to use it for a rendezvous himself, when he grew up and was king-pin of a famous outlaw gang. But Tex had found it, and he liked the use Tex put it to even better—to jail the Box Bar crew!

He hadn't meant to stay when he came up. He thought Tex had killed them, and poked them in there, and he just wanted to see. But he'd found them alive, and they'd hounded him to let them out. Bat Rouge had told him, he'd better, because they had a hole most cut through the rocks, and would be out by morning, anyway. So he'd decided to stand guard till Tex came, and make sure they didn't.

He'd told them that he would shoot the first man to come out, and give them any brand of bullet they preferred! He could, too, for he had all kinds right handy! Snooping around before dark last night, he'd found the heap of guns behind the boulder. The rock had shelved out over them, so they hadn't been snowed under. And he had a regular arsenal around him now.

Propped up there in the midst of his guns, in the nest of boulders facing the dugout, Heck wished Tex would hurry up and get well. For it was pretty hard keeping awake all night. Pretty cold, too—even with a camp fire. And he was hungry enough to eat a raw dog! Besides, he could hear them chipping, chipping, at the rock in there, and had to watch so close. His eyes got tired. Kept—going—shut——

"You young whelp!" he woke with a start to see Bat's face in the window, rage-distorted out of all human cast. "You're monkeyin' with dynamite! I tell you we got this wall most bored through! You let us out, or when I git out, I'll clean up on you. Yeah, an' that Texan, too!"

"Ho-ho-ho!" taunted Heck, behind the gun, little recking the fires he fanned. "*You* clean up on Tex! Yeah, in a pig's eye! Lookit what he done to you! Lookit your face—like you fell under a stampede! *You* lick Tex! Pooh! There ain't men enough in the whole Okanogan to lick Tex!"

Goaded almost beyond endurance at being shamed by a boy, before these men who had seen his defeat, Bat howled, black with fury: "Go bring him here, an' see if he's man enough——"

"That's the stuff!" Kinney applauded. "That's the way to talk to a kid!"

"Bring him here, an' see if he's man enough to unlock that door an' try me again!"

Gee, how Heck wished he could, and make up for the fight he'd missed!

"Where is he?" yelled Bat.

As if he knew just where to hit, to lash this man on the raw, Heck shouted: "He's up to the Box Bar!"

"You lyin' brat!"

Rush Kinney, grayer than any wolf, started forward.

"I ain't lyin'!" denied the boy in satanic glee at the consternation he'd spread—for their excited mutter came out to him, and he'd seen Bat flinch, through the pane. "The women," Heck played up to it, "musta took a big shine to Tex, for they invited him home from the dance! An' he's there now, an' Janice is sure makin' him right at home!"

"He's lyin'!" Kinney swore, as Bat, inarticulate with fury, swung back. "He's tryin' to git our goat—like he's done all night!"

"Don't ever git that in your head," said the former Curly Q man, who had been Hector's pal. "You're hearin' truth."

"If I thought that," Kinney cried hoarsely, wildly pacing his prison, "I'd go mad! The Texan was crazy—the look of him made my blood run cold! If I thought he'd gone down to the ranch—to my wife an' daughter—— *He did!*" The man was wholly distraught. "He's killed Lou an' the rest! That's why they don't come!"

Mojave had the only cool head in the lot. "How would they come?" he argued. "They don't know there *is* such a place. We didn't know it! Bat an' his men followed the Texan here. The Texan tricked Bat's men into the cabin, licked Bat——"

Bat Rouge cursed viciously.

"Licked Bat!" repeated Mojave, with secret relish, "an' threw him in! Then you an' me—who had circled down by Janice's cabin—trailed the rest here, to run into a gun in the hands of a maniac, an' git locked in ourselves. But nobody's goin' to trail *us,* for the snow wiped out every track. Judgin' by the way it piled up on that brush yonder, it snowed a foot or more night before last. If we wait to be found, there won't be much left of us to find! Nobody'll come here in a month of Sundays——"

"I ain't waitin' to be found," gritted Bat Rouge. "I'm gittin' out!"

Tortured by the jealous fear that Tex was at the Box Bar, had been there for three days, improving the time he'd been in hell here, to further his acquaintance with Janice Kinney, Bat resumed his furious attack on the wall. By careful soundings, this spot beside the window had been judged the weakest. But, so far, it had defied the best efforts of all.

All but Bat had given up hope. But he kept steadily chipping at it, nicking, splintering slivers of granite, until he'd used up every knife blade among them, but succeeded, at last, in digging out a good grip for his hand. The wall had been so constructed that the stones wouldn't push out, but if they came, must come inward. Now, in a very frenzy, Bat pulled till his veins stood out purple, and perspiration streamed down his face despite the chill that had taken the heart out of the rest.

Utterly dispirited, his fears for his own fate swallowed up in fear for his family, Rush Kinney slumped down on a bench, and buried his face in his hands. This was what a man came to when he rode hate.

Hate got the bit in its teeth, and a man couldn't stop. Couldn't see what he was riding into. And a man never rode hate alone, but carried his family along with him.

He hated Jeff Hale! Hale had insulted his family, and blackened his name. It had given him a bad name in the country—the things Hale had accused him of. Nobody liked Hale, but trust folks to side with the under dog. Where there was smoke, they said, there was bound to be fire. But he hadn't done one of those things. He wouldn't stampede a man's cows. He wouldn't burn a man's hay! Why, he'd carry the rope to hang a hombre who would! Yet folks thought he'd done those things to Hale. No wonder Hale hated him!

He had intended to run Hale out of the country. That's why he'd held onto Thunder Brakes. If he could keep Hale off until spring, he'd be closed out, and forced to go. He had come up here to do it—drop a few cows, and bluff him out. But——

"Not at the cost of human life," he groaned aloud. "I wouldn't have stood bloodshed!"

Bat Rouge, resting from his labors, eyed him contemptuously. "Bah!" he jeered. "There'd have been blood spilt all over them flats, an' you know it! I didn't come up here for any pink tea with Hale. An' there sure will be bloodshed when I git out!"

Shudderingly, Kinney stared at his foreman. How little you knew a man till you got in a jam with him! He was finding Bat out. Bat got them all into this jam by his fool play, his conceit in his fists. But you'd think to hear him that they were to blame.

To himself, now, Kinney admitted that he never had liked Bat. When Hale fired him years ago and he'd come to the Box Bar, he thought Bat had blabbed too much—even though he had a good right to be sore at Hale. But he'd found out these last three days how Bat had nursed that hate, till it was running wild with him.

Watching him, now, tearing at that wall like a mad beast, that he might get out and fufill the vow he'd made a hundred times since they were penned up here to kill the Texan, Kinney came very near being glad the Texan had locked them up. If they had clashed with the Curly Q, Bat would have killed some one, and he'd have been responsible. He, Kinney, would be a murderer! He'd suffered much, and the end was not yet, but he was spared that——

He sprang to his feet as Bat, with a terrific wrench that vibrated the structure, lost his hold and fell heavily back, yelling with fierce exultance:

"It give! I felt it give! Help me, you shorthorns —a few hard pulls will bring it out!"

With the strength of unexpected hope the men ran to his aid, and the rock, loosened by his persistent efforts, crashed in on the floor. But there was still no opening. The walls were three feet thick, and more stones were between them and freedom. But the entering wedge was in. And, heartened by this, the men fell to breaking up table, bunks, benches, anything that would serve as levers.

Out in the bright dawn, his nerves strung to breaking, the boy shrilled: "Stop! Stop! I'll shoot!"

He mustn't let them break out—they'd kill Tex for locking them in! Tex—sick in bed at the Box Bar!

"Stop!" he screamed. Then his sharp eyes saw the rock beside the window move, and a black hole loom where it had been. Into that hole, true to his promise, he emptied his gun. He heard curses, and, snatching another weapon from the heap, he emptied that, too.

"You think I can't shoot! Ask Mojave! I can shoot like a son of a gun! An' I'll shoot the first man who pokes his nose out of that hole!"

"He will!" Mojave warned them. "An' he'll shoot to kill! He's got more nerve than the bunch of us! Stay back from that hole!"

"Be balked by that cub of a Hale!" Bat snarled, at the risk of his life putting his face to the hole.

"All I got to do," he yelled to the boy, "is to jerk another rock out! I'm givin' you one more chance to open that door!"

He ducked as a bullet smashed through the opening and flattened against the wall. Then, completely berserk, yet with cunning enough not to show his body at the opening, he clawed and yanked, shouting triumph as another rock gave way. The hole was wide enough now to admit the body of a man—a small man.

"Git through!" he thrust Mojave toward it. "The other rocks seem too solid to move. Somebody's got to unbolt the door for the rest of us. He won't shoot *you!*"

"I will, too!" screamed the boy, hearing. "Mojave, I will! Don't *make* me, Mojave! You ain't none of you goin' to git out at Tex! Honest, Mojave, I will—I will—I will!"

His old friend knew he would. He knew that rising hysteria wasn't weakness, but deadly purpose. He knew Heck meant that bullet which pinged on the wall beside him to be a warning. And he took it, leaping back.

"I'll take my chances right here!" he told them grimly.

Cursing him for a coward, Bat tore again at the stones. Nothing could withstand him. And the others were cold with something beside the chill of the place as they watched. Another heave, and another rock crashed inward. And the hole was large enough for him!

As he stood beside it, panting, crouching, as

crouches a beast to spring, Kinney, in sudden alarm, commanded:

"You open that door—an' that's *all* you do! Savvy? You leave the boy alone!"

The face Bat turned on him was so livid that he involuntarily shrank. Bat gathered himself to dive through the hole in the least possible fraction of time.

"Go back!" shrieked the boy, as he suddenly bulked there. "I'll blow you into the middle of next week, Bat! I'll *kill* you——"

Bat was through, and bounding toward him. Heck's gun crashed fire and smoke. Bat half spun, clutching at a flesh wound in his shoulder, then, cursing vilely, twisting, dodging, so that Heck's next two shots went wild, bore down on him, wrested the smoking gun from his grip, and, heedless of the men's horrified shouts, struck the boy a blow that knocked him senseless in the snow. Nor did he stop here. But —crazed by the fire in his shoulder, the unleashed fury stored in three awful days—he kicked the helpless lad once, twice. He drew back his foot to kick again, when Mohave, first to follow in his fear for Heck, threw himself upon him, shouting:

"You dog! You yellow dog!"

Snarling like one, Bat whirled on Mojave, and with the strength and quickness that had made him the best scrapper on Thunder River range, sent his fist crashing into Mojave's face, dropping the man senseless beside the boy he had reached too late to save.

Then, brandishing Hector's gun in the face of Kinney's demands to halt, Bat ran to where the boy's pony waited, and, leaping on, rode off like mad for the Box Bar Ranch!

Halfway down the canyon, he met Scotty galloping toward him with extra horses. For Tex had told his secret with his first conscious breath, and the Box Bar was joyfully awaiting Scotty's return with the men. But Bat didn't stop at his excited hail. He almost ran him down. Didn't seem to see him. *Didn't* see him!

For Bat Rouge was seeing the Texan at the Box Bar, and what he would do to him. And his face was awful with what he saw.

It was so awful, that Janice, eagerly watching for her father, eagerly flying out to meet the first arrival and hear news of him, stopped in her tracks, halfway between the door and Heck's poor little, lathered horse.

"Is the Texan here?" Bat cried thickly, flinging down and coming toward her, his bold, glaring eyes riveted on her face.

His lips curled, as her hand flew to her breast and she did not answer.

She saw blood dripping down his left hand from under his coat sleeve, making red blotches on the snow. But it meant nothing, compared to this new, swift-dawning horror—now when she thought all horror past. She had forgotten that Tex had imprisoned them—that they would be out for vengeance. And Tex was helpless to defend himself. Tex mustn't even be disturbed! For he was getting his first natural sleep, and the doctor said everything depended now on quiet, rest!

"Is the Texan here?" More than wolfish was Bat's sneer.

Still she didn't answer.

He pushed past her, and into the hall, where she caught up with him, clung to him, begging him to be still.

"He's here," she admitted, wild with anxiety. "In the bedroom—sick! Too sick——"

"When I git through with him," swore Bat, "he'll be dead!"

Down the hall he heavily strode, heedless of her clinging weight.

"Bat are you crazy?" she implored, in utter horror. "He's sick! You mustn't go in, I tell you! Hear me—you mustn't go! No! No! No! I won't let you!"

"You can't stop me!" he raved, tearing her arms from about him, throwing her roughly from him. "Nobody can stop me—*now!*"

Then, throwing himself into the parlor, he had just sanity enough to know death when he saw it face to face!

For Dell stood before the closed door of the room where his partner lay. And death quivered in his left hand—as proficient in the use of the gun it held, as had been his broken right. And the threat of death was in his gray eyes, and in his ominous, low-voiced:

"*I'll* stop you, Bat!"

CHAPTER XX

GUNNIN' FOR BAT

BRED on the frontier, Rush Kinney was used to scenes of violence. Of necessity, he had partaken in many. But he always gave the other man an even break. Never could he have killed a man with such equanimity, nor had a pang of regret for it then or later, as he could have killed Bat Rouge. Bat's striking down Mojave—a man of half his strength and size—was a coward's trick. But his attack on the boy—whose only crime had been a childish misconception of the situation, and the manly courage to face it—placed him beyond the pale. It was as well Bat Rouge put himself out of Rush Kinney's reach then!

As he dashed away on the stolen horse, and the men, a little dazed by their sudden liberation, bent over Mojave, Kinney lifted the boy in his arms and carried him into the dugout, laying him gently on the one bench that had escaped destruction.

"Game little kid!" he said huskily, smoothing the boy's hair back with rough tenderness.

His blood leaped hot at sight of the purpling bruise on Heck's cheek, where Bat's fist had landed. Then, as Heck showed signs of coming to, Kinney's blood turned to ice at the memory that Bat was on his way to the Box Bar in that murderous mood.

Running outside, with some wild idea of covering on foot the miles between this lonely canyon and home, he saw Mojave and was haltered to the spot.

The little man had picked himself out of the snow, and was gingerly feeling of his jaw. On his lips was a mirthless grin of self-mockery, which nobody shared. Nobody made any comment. There was about him a deadly coldness that stilled all.

With cold deliberation, he sorted over the heap of guns, his hand closing grimly about his own. Coldly deliberate, he broke it, looked at its loaded chambers, closed it, and spun the cylinders. Then, with cold satisfaction, jammed it in his holster and took note of his audience.

"Bat's gone?" His voice had no shade of emotion. Dumbly, the Box Bar rancher nodded.

"Where's the boy?"

Kinney pointed toward the dugout. He knew exactly what was in Mojave's mind. He knew how futile any effort to dislodge it would be. What Mojave would do, he would do! He was a mighty bad man to rile. And Kinney watched, strangely fascinated, as Mojave went in and bent over Heck.

He saw the sensitive fingers slide gently over the bruised cheek. Saw them probe down his side, under his clothing, wrenching a cry of pain from the boy, when they touched the spot where Bat had so brutally kicked him. And Kinney shivered at the cold glitter in Mojave's eyes. Then——

"Scotty!" his men yelled, and Kinney forgot them both.

For, whirling, he saw his cowboy racing up the canyon, with the saddled, plunging horses in his wake. And his eager demands for news of wife and daughter rang above the frantic cheers.

"Fine as silk, both of 'em!" grinned the cowboy, pulling his horse to a rearing halt in their midst. "Ma's jumpin' sidewise helpin' Mary rustle you a scrumptious feed. An' Janice is plumb lookin' the glass out of the winder for you, boss!"

To head off further questions—for Ma Kinney had put him under oath not to tell a word of what transpired there, till she could prepare her husband—Scotty put in one of his own:

"What's wrong with Bat? Met him out here on a Curly Q hoss, goin' like grim death was after him! Wouldn't even give me the trail sign. An' he sure had blood in his eye!"

Rush Kinney jumped on his horse.

"Mojave!" he sent his big voice booming toward the dugout.

Mojave appeared in the door. "Leave my hoss," he said quietly. "I ain't goin' yet. Might as well tell you, Rush—I'm quittin' the Box Bar now."

"Now see here," Kinney fumed, pulling the rein on his anxiety to be off, "I savvy how you feel—

about workin' under Bat. But it won't be necessary for you to quit, Mojave. I'm firin' Bat the minit I——"

"That won't be necessary either!" the calm response sent a shudder through all.

"What you aim to do, Mojave?" Kinney asked weakly.

"Be my own man, so I can settle my own affairs. First thing, I'm takin' the kid to the Curly Q. His folks'll be worryin'."

Scotty's mouth opened to tell him that the Hales were at the Box Bar, but shut tight, recalling Ma's strict injunction. Then, afraid he couldn't keep it shut all the way back with Kinney, and thinking that he could tell Mojave when the rest were gone, Scotty suggested:

"I'd better go along with Mojave, an' spell him off."

Too impatient to parley longer, Kinney put spurs to his horse.

Fear soon put him far in advance of that eager band. How long had it been after Bat left until Scotty came? Ten minutes? Not more! Bat was riding hard. But his horse was fresher, faster than the boy's pony. He ought to catch up with Bat before he got home. But he was still a quarter mile from the Box Bar when Bat forced his entrance.

So when Rush Kinney jerked his horse to a plunging halt in the home yard, nobody flew to meet him.

Nobody watched for him from window and door. In terror he bounded up the steps, reached for the door-knob, and fell back in a confusion of emotions.

For the door had opened to Bat's broad back. And as Bat steadily backed, Kinney—at a loss to account for this new style of exit—saw the blue-black barrel following him out. At the flashing, natural thought that this was the Texan in control of his home, Kinney's hand dropped to his weapon. But surprise paralyzed it, as the man who held the gun now hove in sight—a gray-eyed, determined, patched-up and crippled young puncher, and a perfect stranger to him!

To cap his astonishment, he saw his own and only daughter backing the strange puncher up. She was looking as he had never seen her look before—vivid, flaming, queenly, in womanly outrage.

"Janice," he bewilderedly roared, "what does this mean? What does this hombre think he's doin'—puttin' my foreman out of my home, at the point of a——"

Janice put a finger to her lips. *"S-s-sh,* dad!" she implored. The fact that Tex's life hung on quiet now, was paramount even to her father's return. "It's Dell," she said softly, though her eyes flashed at Bat. "He's puttin' Bat out for me. Bat came storming down here—bent on trouble. He wouldn't be still. He wouldn't get out. He hurt my wrist—see? And Dell——"

White with anger that his foreman should dare lay a hand on his daughter, Kinney turned on him.

"Git out!" he rasped, pointing a long arm down the highway. "I've seen enough of you in the last three days to last me a lifetime! *Git!*"

"Please, dad!" pleaded the girl. "Oh—hush!"

"Fired, huh?" Bat's face was black and corded with rage. "Fired for fightin' your battles! Fired, for wantin' to git back at the yahoo who's to blame for the last three days! You'd kick a man out hungry—an' crippled to boot? Waal, Kinney, mebbe you won't be so easy, when you hear what's been goin' on here——"

It was the convulsive movement on Dell's part, rather than Janice's entreaties, that shut him up.

"Bat," Kinney's voice shook uncontrollably, "git to the kitchen an' stow away grub to last you to Blue Buttes. Tell Mary to fix up that shoulder you're whinin' about. Then—git! Don't let the grass grow under your feet. For when I hear what my girl's got to say, you may go—feet first! Besides, Mojave's on your trail, an' he'll be here, pronto!"

That was like a sluice of ice water to cool Bat's heated brain. His face grayed, as for the first time he realized the folly of his mad outbreak at the dugout. *Mojave!* He'd rather have the devil on his trail, than that little killer. He'd lost his awe of him up there—when Mojave had been unarmed, and himself armed with two big fists, either of which could crush him, *had* crushed him! Now Mojave was out, with a gun in his fist——

Suffering a complete loss of appetite, muttering a threat to come back and finish what he had started, Bat slunk toward the bunk house.

"Now, my young buck," Kinney turned the lightning of his wrath on Dell, "where do you come in? What in the name of——"

"S-s-sh, dad!" Janice was almost frantic now.

"Is that Texan here? He'll find me anything but *easy!* No loony, Lone Star longhorn can stampede me into a dugout with a gun, keep me prisoner, an' git away with it! If I find he has been here—— *Is he here?"* he roared at cowboy and girl. "What's the matter with you—has the cat got your tongue?"

"My stars, Rush!" said Ma, coming out and shutting the door behind her. "I wish he had yours!"

While Kinney sputtered at that, the Box Bar men came pounding up. And, seeing Dell, whom some recognized as the Texan's partner, they set up such a hullabaloo of question and cross-question, that Janice and Ma, despairing of maintaining quiet and order, begged them to take their noise down off the porch, to the bunk house, *anywhere,* but away from here. Rush Kinney's brain—giddy from his long fast—spun like a top, and he cried aggrievedly to Ma:

"Holy cow! you ain't done a thing but 'shoo' me since I got home! What's wrong here anyway? Why should I allus be shoo——"

"We shooed for you," Ma firmly retorted, "when you was sick!"

Kinney looked at her queerly. "Ma, who's sick?"

"The Texan," bravely she met his look. "Rush, come in."

Taking his hand, she lead the dazed rancher inside. Her heart beat wildly under her calico gown. Always, she had been able to "get around" Rush. But this was a man's game. Would he listen to her now? Could she soften his heart toward the Texan who had imprisoned him? Toward Jeff Hale, whom he had so bitterly hated for years? How could she explain the presence of both? Well, one thing at a time and that done well, was a very good rule, Ma Kinney knew. She'd begin with Tex.

At the bedroom door—the one that lead into it through the hall, for Jeff Hale was asleep in the parlor, and she must avoid that room as if it had a plague—Ma stopped to warn him to make no demonstration, when she saw new cause for alarm. Dell was right behind her, as determined to protect Tex from Rush Kinney as he had been from Bat. He hadn't a gun drawn on Kinney, but he had it handy, and his purpose was plain on his pale, set face.

"Dell," Ma said gently, "go back. I want to talk alone with Rush. He won't touch Tex. He won't make a sound."

"How the heck do you know I won't?" fumed the

rancher. He knew Ma was boss, but didn't care about the news getting around.

"You can trust that to me, Dell," said Ma.

And thinking how much he'd already safely trusted to her, Dell did.

June sprang up from the bedside as they entered. Her eagerness to ask Kinney about her brother crowding out any thought that his presence might mean danger to Tex. But before she could speak, Ma whispered kindly:

"Go out to Dell, June," eliminating her, too, from the scene.

Rush Kinney looking down on Tex, could hardly believe he was the man who had trapped him. For the sleeping face, fresh-shaven, so utterly relaxed, bore little resemblance to the wild, bloody countenance that had horrified Kinney then, and haunted his memory since. Pain was gone from that face, but its scars were left. And a great weakness was there, that was a better protection from a right-minded man than even Dell's gun.

"He's been so near death, poor boy," Ma whispered. "Rush, he was out of his head with fever when he locked you up. He wasn't responsible. We brought him here to care for him, because I—I couldn't let him die, and maybe never know—where you were, Rush. He wasn't able to tell us until this morning."

Rush Kinney's eyes lifted to Ma. Her face was

marked, too, with suffering. She'd fought for this man's life—for *him*. That thought, the reaction of being home and finding his loved ones safe, had a softening influence on him.

"Rush"—Ma had been doing some thinking herself—"this boy almost caught his death puttin' those cows on Thunder Brakes. We're to blame for it! We didn't want that land—really. And as far as I can see," Ma killed two birds with one stone, "we've been as stubborn as Hale."

Sure now of her ability to control the next situation, she lead him back in the hall to tell him of Hale. Then, to her dismay, she saw Hale coming toward them. She saw her husband stiffen to see his arch-enemy here, and snort, like one hostile animal meeting another, and she could almost see his iron-gray mane uprear.

Endless the moment to Ma, June and Dell, in which the two old foes regarded each other.

Then, deep on the hush, resounded the Curly Q rancher's husky, uncertain:

"Heaven be thanked!"

And, as Rush Kinney glared dumbly at that:

"Heaven be thanked," Hale cried tremulously, "that you're safe, Rush!"

It was a long time before Kinney found voice, and then it was a cold voice he found. "That's strange talk from you, Jeff Hale!"

Hale's white head bent sorrowfully. "It is," he

owned humbly, "an' more's the shame! But hear me, before you judge me, Rush. Hear my story, an' see why I can't hold enmity toward any man. I've apologized to your daughter. She's been big enough to forgive the thing that started this row. Now, I'm apologizin' to you for the dirt I done you—fencin' them springs. Under the circumstances, Rush, I don't blame you for burnin' my hay, an'——"

"Jeff, you think I done that! You mean to say you actually *think* I burned your hay? Why, good heavens, man, I swear——"

He broke off at a loud commotion outside. Boots clamored on the porch, rang over the threshold.

"Likely the search party," Ma presumed, rushing to quell it. "I sent word you'd been found——"

The door burst open, and Scotty's terrified face peered down the hall.

"Boss, git out here on the double-quick! Mojave's gunnin' for Bat!"

As Kinney stamped out, the Curly Q members pounced upon Hector, who had followed the cowboy in. June caught him up in her arms, hugging him, kissing the bruise on his cheek, to his intense inner comfort, but outward disgust.

"Aw, I ain't a baby!" he sobbed on her neck. "Even if he did lick me. He licked Mojave, too!"

Jeff Hale stiffened at that, and a flame shone in his eyes, so long dead to fire.

"Who hit you, son?"

"Bat!" Heck looked around proudly. "But it took the best scrapper on the range—next to Tex—to do it! He hit me here! See? An' he kicked the stuffin out of me. See—it's all black an' blue already. There'll be green in it to-morrow——"

But Jeff Hale, too, had gone to find Bat.

He found him backed up against the bunk house by Mojave, and immediately fell under the spell that had gripped the entire outfit, massed at the scene. Though Bat was a hideous sight, crouching there, with hate and fear in all their primal nakedness depicted on his swarthy face, in every line of his huge body, it was Mojave, who held their spellbound gaze.

For the little man was little no longer. A terrible power, terrible purpose, added cubits to his stature. He dominated Bat Rouge, dominated all, as he "settled his own affairs," according to the old feud of the West. A code which forbade the interference of any one, as long as the odds were equal.

"See this, Bat!" keeping his cold eye on Bat, he significantly indicated the gun in his holster. "It's the great leveler! It makes up the difference nature put in us. I'm as big as you are now, an' we're goin' to fight!"

"I won't!" Bat's voice was a wail of terror.

"You won't want to," Mojave was relentless, "but I'm goin' to *make* you! But first, you're comin' clean. I've been watchin' you, Bat, for two years now. You'll be surprised how much I've learned!"

Sheer panic swept the Box Bar foreman.

"Hale," Mojave changed neither his tone nor position, "listen in on this. You, too, Rush. You'll git a earful!"

Wonder intensifying their strain, the two old ranchers stepped nearer. And, Mojave, watching Bat like a hawk, addressed himself to his old employer.

"Hale, you been wonderin' who stampeded your cows after the springs was fenced?"

"No, by heaven!" Jeff Hale denied hotly. "I know it was Bat!"

Rush Kinney's voice rose above Bat's strangled protest, but Mojave swept aside both.

"Correct!" he approved. "I know, too! I was ridin' range with Bat at the time. We parted trails that day, an' when we joined up again, he crowed he'd done it."

"It's a lie!" shrilled Bat.

"Hale," Mojave might not have heard that either, "you been wonderin' who burnt your hay last fall?"

"No!" roared Hale, enraged at the memory. "We tracked Bat from the stack to the Box Bar!"

"It's a lie!" Wildly Bat's eyes beseeched Kinney to back him up, but the rancher was shocked beyond all speech.

"Correct!" Mojave approved again. "Mebbe there ain't much I can tell you, after all. Hale, do you know who beat you up down in Spokane, an' robbed you of the money you'd mortgaged your ranch to raise?"

"I do," hope leaped to Bat's eyes as Hale began, "it was a sail——"

Then his jaw clamped down on the word, for it wasn't necessary to use a pick ax now to remove an idea from Jeff Hale's head.

Some one snickered hysterically, for this was a standing joke in the country. And even Mojave faintly grinned.

"It was Bat! I can prove it——"

"It's a lie!" Bat screamed, shaking all over in a convulsion of terror and hate. "He's lyin', I tell you! He——"

"Hale," in steely tone, Mojave cut in, "you're goin' wasn't any secret here. We knew why you were goin', an' how much money you carried. The day after you left, Bat asked for a lay off. Wanted to visit a sick pal up on Tunk Creek, he said. Am I right, Rush?"

"So far," Kinney admitted in dread.

"An' while he was gone, Hale was knocked out an' robbed! Well, I had a suspicion—knowin' Bat probably better than any of you. An' I wrote to my ol' bunkie, who happens to be foreman of the Triple X, Bat! He said you hadn't been there. Said he'd never heard of you, nor had any of his men. But he said he remembered a hombre of your description *did* ride in town on a big black, which he left at the livery stable, an' took the train to Spokane!"

"It's a lie, I tell you!" Bat frothed.

"They can check up on it—after!" Mojave was watching Bat with terrible intensity now. "My pard, up there, found out for me that you came back three days later on the train, got your horse an' started for Thunder River range the night of the blizzard——"

"You—you——"

Dell, who had followed Hale out, in wrath over the attack on Heck, to remain an awed spectator, now became an active participant.

"I can check you up on that!" he told Mojave, as Bat turned livid and settled in his crouch. "Tex an' me were at the stable when he rode in. Curious will back us up! Bat knocked a train check out of his hat, an' Tex has got it! We can easy prove——"

"Thanks, pard," Mojave said softly, "we won't need to. In half a minute I'll tell you why."

A terrible suspicion, borne all along, became a more terrible certainty to Bat. Abject terror seized him, and with it the courage that comes with despair. He must get out, or still that tongue. He couldn't get out——

"Bat," in his final denouncement, Mojave seemed to grow by leaps and bounds, filling the bright and sunlit space with his awful presence, "Bat, you've done everything a man could do to make trouble for Hale.

You've let Rush Kinney in for arson—an' worse. You've rode roughshod over this range, because no man would call your time. But it ain't for them things, *I'm* callin' you. It's because you beat up a kid that calls Mojave pal! Knocked him out—kicked him when he was down! You're too accursed mean to encumber the earth! Bat, you've got Hale's money sewed in your clothes right now——"

Bat's hand hitched to his gun—fatally!

The explosion crashed deafeningly on the strung nerves of the women, within. Then it died away into silence—dead, profound.

But, as if it were a lullaby to insure the sleep that was life itself, the convalescent Texan slumbered on.

CHAPTER XXI

DELL'S LONELINESS

BAT ROUGE was gone! Gone, forever, from the range he had ridden roughshod; tramped so ruthlessly in his No. 10 boots. And the air was purer, the sun brighter, and every one better for his going.

Mojave, with a last wave, last "Adois!" was gone—speeded by the tearful prayers of his kid pal, Heck, and the good wishes of all who knew him.

"Reckon he'll hit for the border," decided the sheriff, who, with the returning search party, rode in on the echo of that shot. "Waal, I'd best be after him."

"Why?" Kinney was still quivering with righteous wrath, that his foreman had made him guilty of all the crimes Jeff Hale had accused him of. "Mojave shot in self-defense. We'll all swear to that!"

"Jist the same," said the conscientious officer, "I'll have to bring him back."

Still—considering that the Canadian border was only a score of miles away—he evinced no great haste to be about it.

"You say Mojave said the money was on Bat?" he asked. "Hale, could you identify it?"

"There was ten one-hundred-dollar bills," the Curly Q rancher explained, "in the bill fold June give me for Christmas—black, with my initials in gold."

Under their tense gaze, the sheriff made a search of the dead man's clothing. Sure enough, eventually a fat, black, initialed bill fold turned up!

"That yours, Hale?" he held it out. "Got your initials—J. H. See?"

"Looks like it!" admitted Hale joyfully.

"A-huh!" ejaculated the officer, examining its contents. "Ten one hundreds! Hale, this is sure lucky for you. But, of course, I'll have to keep it, you savvy, till after this case is investigated."

This settled, the sheriff lighted a cigarette and turned to Kinney. "Now, Rush, yould you mind tellin' me where you was, while I been ridin' my hoss to death huntin' you?"

So Kinney told him of their confinement in the lonely dugout, which, he declared, "it would take a crazy man or a kid to find!" And the sheriff, running through the files of memory, recollected one "Dry Creek" Johnson, a horse thief, who operated in that section years ago, and had a hidden hangout in the Thunder Brakes region, to which he was wont to retreat when the Vigilantes were pressing him hard. He reckoned Johnson had built the dug out. And he wondered how the Texan had ever stumbled onto it.

Hale, then, explained that he had a line cabin a mile west of the dugout, where Tex had intended to stop.

But, in his delirious condition, he had blundered into the wrong canyon, and found the dugout instead. It took a lot of explanation to make everything perfectly clear to the sheriff, who had never struck his constituents as being an obtuse fellow before.

But at last he drawled, "I'd best be hittin' Mojave's trail," putting his toe in the stirrup and giving his body a heave. "Glad everything's turned out so fine here for everybody. Waal, so long, folks!"

"He's been *so long,*" Kinney grinned, as his broad back bobbed away, "that a slow hoss could have made a start that Man-o'-War couldn't cut down. Boys, Mojave's safe!"

Now, in spite of this lengthy discussion and all, the dinner Ma Kinney had prepared for her famished husband and crew hadn't even had time to get cold. So—as the last sign of tragedy was borne from the Box Bar—they all went in to dinner. For it would take more than a tragedy to blunt the ravenous appetites these men had acquired in their three-day fast.

For the first time in their long feud, Rush Kinney and Jeff Hale kicked their boots under the same table.

"Rush, I've been a stubborn ol' fool!" Jeff Hale abused himself.

"Jeff, at your worst, you wasn't a patch on me!" Kinney went him one better.

They kept on calling themselves names, each trying

to outdo the other, while Janice and June, nervous and shaken by the sad occurrence, chattered twice as fast in an effort to forget it, covering the years of their forced separation.

But Dell, who had stayed to dinner at everybody's insistence, ate little and said less. There wasn't anything for him to say, and nobody to say it to. He felt lonelier than when he had been alone. And he decided not to stay and be a "wet blanket." He'd go over to the Curly Q and pack up. Tex was too weak to have company yet. So he'd get all ready, and come over to-morrow and say good-by to Tex.

Excusing himself, when they all left the table, he went to the barn. Lou saddled his horse. And Dell swung up, pulled it about, and headed down the Box Bar drive——

"Dell!" Had he been gone a month, that voice would have reached him!

Riding back to the porch where June waited for him, Dell smiled determinedly. He was determined to cast no cloud over her day. But something in his smile, something about him—sitting there in the saddle, his forehead still bandaged, his arm bound over his breast—brought tears to June's eyes. She ran down the steps and caught his bridle, nervously toying with it, as she spoke.

"Dell," her voice shook more than a little, "you'll be back to-morrow? Tex will be able to talk to you then. Promise you'll come over the first thing in the morning, Dell!"

"Sure!" That was easy. He meant to. He wouldn't go without seeing Tex.

Earnestly June watched him ride off in the sun, his spurs jingling merrily, his blue bandanna fluttering out—a jaunty figure for all his crippled arm. On the crest he turned and stood in the stirrups to wave his sombrero to her, and show her how fine everything was with him.

Then he rode over the hill. And with the hill between, and no need to act, all the jauntiness went out of Dell. He slumped, his pace slowed, muting his spur's merry jingle. And the white-and-gold, sunny valley he rode, was an empty casket, rifled of every dream.

Some folks said love wasn't anything much. Love was *everything!* Everything was nothin, without love. Still, he'd always have something. He'd always have his own love for June. Love didn't need to be loved back to make it worth while. He'd always be glad he came to the Curly Q. He'd always be glad it was Tex that June loved. Tex had always been so kind of alone and unhappy—— Well, Tex would be happy now. Everybody was happy! Even the cows——

For he could see the Curly Q herd down in the feed yard, munching away Box Bar hay, or standing about in the mellow sunshine—tottery, still, but all fed up—chewing their cuds—plumb happy!

And down there, knee-deep in a rick of alfalfa, old Calliope was pitching hay in the racks, bellowing—happy:

"Oh, I went down South for to see my gal,
Sing Polly Wolly Doodle all the day!
My Sal, she is a spunky gal,
Sing——"

"Great snakes, Cal!" objected Dutch, with even more than the old-time spirit—proving that he was happy, too, "shut up that infernal racket! Let's count our blessin's, Cal. Our boss is plumb humanized. Our cows is saved. Tex is gittin' well. An' I'll eat my shirt, boots an' bandanna, if we don't have a weddin'——"

Yeah, everything had turned out fine for everybody!

Then why did Dell's lean jaw quiver as he packed his suit case in the bunk house, to strike out on his own—for Texas, maybe? What blinded his eyes, making him run into his bunk? And what made him slide down beside it, his good arm stretched across it, and that fist slowly clench and unclench? And what, with his face buried there, shook his slim body, shook every fiber of him?

"Everybody—happy? *Yeah!*"

CHAPTER XXII

OVER THE SKY LINE

TRUE to his promise to June, Dell rode over to the Box Bar next morning—a morning memorable to Thunder River Range, every cattle range in the Okanogan, every range in the great Northwest.

June met him at the door, and took him in. Not as she had last time—as if she were sorry for him. But as if—he didn't know what. He'd never seen her like that—so nervous and flurried—telling him he musn't stay long, mustn't excite Tex, mustn't let Tex talk too much——

Then Dell was in the bedroom, looking down at his partner, and his heart jumped up in his throat, and he couldn't say a thing! Tex couldn't either. Their eyes said a lot, though, and so did their hands in that long grip. He grinned at Tex, and Tex grinned back—the old Tex!

Yeah, he was just the same, for all that he'd have to stand twice in the same place—say he *could* stand—to cast a shadow. The reckless look had gone out of his face. The hungry light had gone out of his eyes—eyes that weren't so big and bright now, but natural, happy, as if Tex had found trail's end at last.

Dell wanted to tell Tex how glad he was about that. Then break it easy about his going away. But it was hard to say either. So he sat down in the chair by the bed, swinging his sombrero between his knees, trying not to see June fussing around Tex, trying to think of some way——

"Sam Houston!" Tex cussed—natural as life but weak, lifting a thin hand to the soft wind billowing through the open window. "Feels jist like summer, Dell!"

Glad to have something cheerful to tell, Dell stepped to the window.

"Take a look, Tex!" he cried, pulling the curtain aside.

Tex's dark head turned on the pillow, and his dark, wondering eyes journeyed out to the transformed world—a lavender world. Stained with the diluted hue of the purple-black cloud that had come rolling up from the South in the night, spreading over the range; swathing the hills in deep-lavender mists; veiling, in lavender, the face of the sun, so it wouldn't be shamed by the working of a magic greater than its own. And a curious rushing filled the air—the soft swish made by millions of evergreens slipping their burdens and springing erect; the swirl of Badger Creek, already unchained, running full-banked with melted snows.

"Tex, it's the Chinook!" Dell answered the wonder in Tex's eyes. "To-morrow night the snow will be gone! Spring's here! Ol' winter's dead!"

The Texan's face flooded with great content.

"I licked it!" he proudly grinned. "I licked the winter. It give me a hard jolt or two, but it's dead, an' I'm still in the ring. Dell, I won't be afraid of winter again."

Glad of this, too, Dell sat down again. If Tex was going to make his home up here—— That was *three* times June had fluffed up his pillow since he came in!

"Reckon all hands'll be busy," Tex grinned—eager, you could see, to get out, "pullin' weak cows outta the mud now—instead of the snow!"

Dell saw a break in the fence, and lunged for it. "Yeah," he crossed his legs, hoping he sounded offhand, "but I reckon I won't stay for the spring work, Tex. Reckon I'll pull out—don't want to leave all my hoof prints on one range."

Tex looked at June, and she started fluffing up that pillow again. But Dell caught her whisper:

"Tex, you tell him now!"

"Oh, he ain't goin' so quick as all that!" Tex teased her, in a way that stabbed Dell all over again, and made June blush like a rose and run out of the room.

And Dell braced himself to hear Tex tell it. He *had* to look happy. He had to smile. He could stand anything for a minute or two——

"Pard," Tex's tone was mighty serious and so was his thin face against the white pillow, "I got something to tell you. It's something I ought to have told you long ago. I know now, my *not* tellin' has made you see things different from what they was. But I—I was so touchy about it, an'—ashamed to tell you, Dell."

"Don't tell me, Tex, if you'd rather not."

"But I want to, pard," Tex's weak voice was eager. "I ain't ashamed of it *now!* Recollect that night in Blue Buttes, when I told you it was a family matter that brought me North? The truth is, Dell, I come up to hunt my family. You see, my parents had trouble, an' my home was broke up, when I was jist eight. My dad was a mighty hard man—narrow as a boot lace, stubborn as a mule, an' jealous of his shadow. My mother was an angel, or she couldn't have stood him as long as she did. But there was a limit to what she could stand. And she reached it one night, when he got jealous because she wanted to go over to a neighbor's house to a dance—not over her goin', mind, but jist *wantin'* to go! He flew into such a tantrum that she had to leave him. An' she took her two children—my baby sister an' me—down to El Pas'."

Dell stared at Tex, divining, rejecting in fear that which he divined.

"Mother went to work, Dell, supportin' us kids as best she could. Dad sold out, an' followed her there. Not to make up—he was too stubborn for that—but to sneak in the house, when she was at work an' I was at school, an' steal my baby sister from her ol' Mexican nurse! That was the last time we ever saw either of them. Mother's heart broke, an' she died in a year. I know now that dad tried to locate me after he heard of her death, but I'd been taken to another part of the State."

Gently the Chinook stirred Tex's dark hair, swept from his face the pain of remembering.

"Naturally, Dell, I never had any use for my dad. But I grew up, wantin' my sister. Wantin' a home—kin—somebody to love! I set out to find her. It was a long, long trail, but I found her at last! Found dad, too! And there was the rub—that was why I didn't tell you——"

Dell's eyes were looking straight through him now, and his face was white as a sheet.

"Pard, grab the saddle horn," Tex gave warning, "for I'm goin' to pitch! *June is my sister!* I knew it when she came into the depot that night. I'd have canceled my ticket to heaven to help her! Ain't she sweet, Dell? Yeah, I remember you said so that night of the blizzard. But I wasn't in any hurry to own dad—Jeff Hale—after the way he treated us—seein' how he was treatin' her—like he had treated my mother.

"But I—I couldn't keep from tellin' June, Dell. I bogged down an' told her that night you saw us—

out at the horse corral. I told her not to tell you, till I could tell you myself. Then I got sick, an' I couldn't. She told dad an' the rest, when they thought I was—goin' west. But she wouldn't let them tell you."

Did joy kill? Dell had heard that it didn't, but he was sure it was killing him! Tex hadn't broken his pledge to Jeff Hale or him. Tex was as true as the North Star—true as the truest thing in the world. Tex was his partner still! And June——

"Dad an' me," Tex went on with a note of deep feeling, "have had a talk. He's plumb changed, Dell. I've changed toward him. He didn't suffer jist one year, but *every* year! He hid his sufferin', like I hid my shame of him, an' it kept him mean. But when June told him about me it was the last straw, an' it broke him up. He's so sorry—an' blood's thicker than water, Dell! I'm plumb proud of him now. I'm Tex Hale from now on—Rankin was the name of the man who raised me. An', pard——"

A strange radiance lighted the face of Tex, a strange reverence throbbed in his tone, "I'll be up in a week or so, an' I'm goin' home, Dell—*home!*"

"To Texas?" Dell's lips moved mechanically.

"No, you moony yahoo, to the Curly Q! With my sister, dad, an' the gamest li'le scout that ever trod shoe leather, my half-brother, Heck!"

So it wasn't good-by that Dell said to June in the Box Bar parlor, with his good arm around her, and her sweet face—pinker, prettier than he'd ever seen it—looking right into his, and his heart running wild. He said the farthest thing from good-by. He said —— Well, what they all say!

Two months have passed. The war—in which man was allied with brute against Nature—is ended. The weaklings, both man and brute, are gone. All that are left, are strong. And the frozen range has thawed and flowered—the more gorgeously for the unusual severity of the season passed, as is ever Nature's remorseful, beautiful recompense.

Vividly blue, the summering columbine in the thickets. Summer winds sing sweet requiem in the fragrant grasses for the winter killed. And in the grasses prairie dogs who have slept the winter, tumble and play. Calves playfully kick up their heels, who know not winter yet. And on the sky line, cowboys, who have beaten the winter, ride easy and free.

Who are these riders on the sky line this fragrant May twilight—here, on the hill, between the Box Bar and the little schoolhouse on Badger Creek? This lean, sinewy, dark-eyed cowboy, this black-eyed girl, riding up on the sky line, their horses reined close?

"Dad says," the girl's happy laugh was a joy to hear, "we ought to be able to hold Thunder Brakes with a homestead and lease on it both!"

"An' a *home!*" happily reminded the man. Don't forget that! Janice, when I think you an' I will be married one week from to-day, an' livin' over on Thunder Brakes——"

"Tex, you're mussing my hair!"

"Who cares? You allus look pretty to me! That's all you care about, ain't it?"

"Watch out, Tex, or you'll be getting jealous. You know what——"

"*Jealous?* Girl, I'm that jealous, I——"

Then they dropped over the sky line.

And, lo and behold, right where they have been, is a team and buckboard. One that has gone out of its way to drop Jeff Hale off at the Box Bar, so he could "chew the rag with Rush," while the young folks enjoyed themselves.

"Oh, Dell, I can't believe this is me—going, *really!*" —a sweetly excited girlish voice. "Listen, Dell, I hear the music——"

"June, I ain't listenin' to a thing, but you! I'm loco about you! An' to think I got you, an' my partner, too! Everything *sure* turned out fine for every——"

Then they dropped over the sky line, too.

Who is this little figure, looming up here on a little bay pony to stop on the sky line, and look at the romancing four just ahead, and wheel his horse?

"Aw, mush!" That disgusted treble can only be

Heck's! "I'm goin' back to the bunk house an' chin with Lou. *He* ain't got the girl bug—yet."

More riders, more buckboards, follow by scores. But you don't catch any of them going back! For there's a big dance at the schoolhouse to-night. Everybody is turning out—as light-hearted and gay, as if there never had been, never would be again, the white days, the grim phase, of Thunder River Range before the Chinook.

THE END.

Cherry Wilson enjoyed a successful career as a Western writer for twenty years. She produced over two hundred short stories and short novels, numerous serials, five hardcover books, and six motion pictures were based on her fiction. Readers of *Western Story Magazine,* the highest paying of the Street & Smith publications where Wilson was a regular contributor, held her short stories in high regard. Wilson moved from Pennsylvania with her parents to the Pacific Northwest when she was sixteen. She led a nomadic life for many years and turned to writing fiction when her husband fell ill. The first short story she sent to *Western Story Magazine* was accepted, and this began a long-standing professional relationship. If thematically Wilson's Western fiction is similar to that of B. M. Bower, stylistically her stories are less episodic and, as her experience grew, exhibit a greater maturity of sensibility. Her early work, especially, parallels Bower rather closely in that she developed a series of interconnected tales about a group of ranchhands. There is also a similar emphasis on male bonding and comedic scenes. Wilson stressed human relationships in preference to gun play and action. In fact, some of her best work can be found in those stories that deal with relationships between youngsters and men, as in her novel, *Stormy* (1929), and short stories such 'Ghost Town Gold' which has been collected in *The Morrow Treasury of Great Western Short Stories* (1997). Three of Wilson's novels served as the basis for the Buck Jones production unit at Universal Pictures in the 1930s. *Empty Saddles* (1929) and *Thunder Brakes* (1929), book publications of serials first appearing in *Western Story Magazine,* are among her finest Western novels. A collection of her best Western short novels and stories is currently being prepared for **Five Star Westerns**.